KU-033-458

STORNOWAY

PUFFIN BOOKS

THE MINERVA PROGRAM

When Minerva gets picked to go on a computer course she knows this is her big chance to excel, to be really good at something. As she looks at the words on the screen she is filled with satisfaction. To this terrific machine sitting in front of her she is the most important person in the world, the *only* person in the world, and that feels good.

But things take a turn for the worse when Minerva is accused of cheating the system and is removed from the computer class. Minerva had been set up, there's no doubt about it. But who would want to do such a thing and why? She is determined to find the culprit and solve the mystery. Together with her little brother 'Spiderman' and her best friend Sophie, she devises the foolproof Minerva Program.

A cleverly written story, full of humour and surprise which will appeal to computer nuts everywhere.

Claire Mackay lives in Toronto, and works freelance as a writer and research librarian. She has published many books for young people, including the award-winning *One Proud Summer*.

The Minerva Program

Claire Mackay

PUFFIN BOOKS
in association with
Oxford University Press

PUFFIN BOOKS

Published by the Penguin Group
27 Wrights Lane, London W8 5TZ, England
Viking Penguin Inc., 40 West 23rd Street, New York, New York 10010, USA
Penguin Books Australia Ltd, Ringwood, Victoria, Australia
Penguin Books Canada Ltd, 2801 John Street, Markham, Ontario, Canada L3R 1B4
Penguin Books (NZ) Ltd, 182–190 Wairau Road, Auckland 10, New Zealand

Penguin Books Ltd, Registered Offices; Harmondsworth, Middlesex, England

First published in Canada by James Lorimer and Company 1984
First published in Great Britain by Oxford University Press 1987
Published in Puffin Books 1990
1 3 5 7 9 10 8 6 4 2

Copyright © Claire Mackay, 1984
All rights reserved

Filmset in Century Schoolbook

Printed and bound in Great Britain by
Richard Clay Ltd, Bungay, Suffolk

Except in the United States of America, this book is sold subject
to the condition that it shall not, by way of trade or otherwise, be lent,
re-sold, hired out, or otherwise circulated without the publisher's
prior consent in any form of binding or cover other than that in which
it is published and without a similar condition including this condition
being imposed on the subsequent purchaser.

To my son Ian, in gratitude
for his help and advice
...and so much more

1

"JAMES!"

Where was he? Five minutes to catch the bus and he disappears. As usual, thought Minerva.

"James! Come on!"

She ran to the kitchen. It was a mess. His turn to clean up. Which he'd conveniently forgotten. Again as usual. Moving fast, she put the milk and butter in the fridge and stacked the dishes in the sink. A breeze fluttered the roll of paper towels.

"Balcony," she whispered. In three long strides she was through the open door and staring at her nine-year-old brother, two metres below at the fourth floor. He was climbing down the building again, slowly playing out the yellow nylon rope tied to the iron railing in front of her.

"James, you come on up!"

He shook his head. "Can't. I'm practising."

Sighing, Minerva reeled him in until he flopped over the railing into her arms. He was small and light for his age, and she held him easily.

"You got something against elevators?" she asked.

James nodded. "They're boring."

"They're also faster than a rope — and we've got exactly four minutes. Move it!" She set him on his feet and he dashed away.

"Wait for me! You know what..." The apartment door slammed in the middle of her sentence. "... Mom said!"

She grabbed her knapsack and ran, with a nagging sense she'd forgotten something. But she couldn't stop now. She checked the lock and hurried down the corridor.

James lay stretched out, corpse-like, his head and feet keeping the elevator doors open. His eyes were closed and his hands folded as if in prayer.

Minerva had a sudden vision of a dozen neighbours on other floors jabbing angrily at the "Down" button. She nudged James with the toe of her North Star. "Get up, spaz!" He didn't move. She nudged harder. "James, get up!"

"Can't. I'm dead."

"I should be so lucky." She stepped over him, then swiftly bent and tickled him. He jack-knifed into giggles and rolled towards her, and the steel doors shuddered to a close. Minerva pressed "Lobby," then pinned James to the wall by leaning on him. The elevator rocked its way down to the third floor. A woman carrying a little brown dog got on. The dog looked at them and growled. James growled back. Minerva leaned harder on him and pretended to read the graffiti. "E.T. CALL YOUR ANSWERING SERVICE." "Rosa loves Frank," in purple lipstick. Ha! thought Minerva. She also loves Joe, Freddy, and Nick. Wonder if Frank knows.

The elevator stopped at two. Mrs. B. got on, wearing what looked like an awning. Mrs. B. — her name had about eighteen syllables and a couple of hyphens, so Minerva had long ago given up on it — was big. Very big. And she held in front of her a large laundry hamper.

From behind Minerva James said, "Hi, Mrs. B."

Mrs. B. looked around and smiled, then nodded mistily at the wall and tightened her grip on the hamper. It gurgled. Minerva grinned. Mrs. B. was off to the laundry room with her usual daily load: three sheets, a can of V-8 juice, and a bleach bottle full of vodka.

They lurched to a stop at the lobby, and the doors slid apart. Minerva and James moved forward. The little brown dog barked, a high squawking noise like a chicken. James squawked back. It was a good imitation. The short woman frowned and said, "Go walkies, angel!", and the dog barked again. So did James. Mrs. B. just stood there, smiling and nodding like the Queen on a Royal Tour.

Minerva spied the bus and ran, James right behind her barking at every step. The little brown dog leaped out of the short woman's arms and ran squawking after them. The short woman brought up the rear, waving a leash and yelling, "Walkies, angel! Walkies!"

"James, why?" Minerva asked as they darted through the crisp October sunlight and swung aboard the bus. "Why do you do stuff like that?"

"Doesn't that dog like black people, or what? He a racist, man? Soon as he saw us he started to bark!"

"Get real, James! Who ever heard of a racist dog? Besides, dogs are colour-blind. And why can't we go to school like normal regular people for once?"

"Trouble with you, Minnie, you got no sense of humour." He wriggled into the small space behind the driver and ignored her.

Minerva lowered her voice. "You call me Minnie once more, James, and I tear out your tongue and roast it on a stick."

He jerked his head towards her, and his eyes widened.

"And then make you eat it," she added.

She felt much better after that and worked her way down the aisle towards the back. Good. Sophie had saved her a place. She tripped over a grade eight boy plugged into his Walkman and fell into the cold vinyl seat.

"Hi, Soph. Thanks."

Sophie's clever dark eyes filled with tears.

"Was it something I said?" asked Minerva.

Sophie shook her head, swallowed hard, and then pointed to the book in her lap. *The Old Curiosity*

Shop," read Minerva, "by Charles Dickens. So?"

"Little Nell just died," said Sophie.

"Oh," said Minerva. "Was it sudden?"

"No. I knew she would." Sophie blew her nose.

"What's the next book? Maybe it's not as sad," said Minerva. Sophie was working her way through Dickens alphabetically.

Sophie held up another book. "*Oliver Twist*. I think he's alive at the end. But not before he gets into all kinds of trouble."

Minerva grunted. "I know the type."

"James goofing around again?"

"Honest, Soph, he's such a drag sometimes! He should be kept in a cage!"

Sophie grinned and settled back. "What'd he do today?"

Minerva told her, and even before the part about the barking contest Sophie started to laugh. Minerva looked at her and laughed, too. Her mood lightened. Funny how Soph could always do that. She felt a rush of warmth. She hadn't had too many friends, especially since they'd moved, almost a year ago now, from the little flat on St. Clair way out here to a high-rise on the eastern edge of the city. She'd felt all alone for months, then one day Sophie sat beside her on the bus, just like today. They had laughed about something. Just like today. And they'd been friends ever since.

The bus wheezed to a stop in front of Pinevale Senior and its feeder school, Sir Ernest Macmillan Elementary, where James was in grade four. The kids crowded out. Minerva noticed the new girl with the punk haircut and the green eyeshadow hanging on Mark Hofmann like a Christmas decoration. Guess he dumped Patricia Leach, she thought. Can't think of anyone who deserves it more. Then Mark turned up his shoulder stereo, and she couldn't hear what Sophie was saying.

"What?!" she yelled.

Mark turned a corner.

"I said I'll see you in gym!" Sophie yelled back.

Minerva stopped in her tracks. "I think I'll kill myself!"

"What's wrong?"

"I forgot my gymsuit!"

"Oh, Minerva, not again!"

"It's my dumb brother's fault!"

"Pickle will freak right out, Min. That's the third time this month!"

"Aaargh!" groaned Minerva. "I wonder if you can fail gym."

"You'll be the first to know."

"Thanks a lot."

Sophie waved and turned into Mrs. Olivetti's class. Minerva walked on, sunk in gloom, to her own home-room at the end of the hall. Mr. Guthrie was already there, rummaging through his desk. Minerva smiled in spite of her worry. He was really a nice guy and a good teacher — but sometimes he couldn't even remember what year it was. Some of the kids ran a weekly pool on how many things he'd forget. You paid a quarter, picked a number from one to a hundred, and whoever came closest got the money. Last week Eric Johansen had won seven dollars for guessing thirty-three.

She slipped into her seat. Day Two. Math first. That was a break anyway.

The bell. *O Canada*. Announcements. Maybe gym was cancelled, she thought with a surge of hope. Maybe somebody swiped Miss Dill's green jogging suits. No wonder we call her Pickle. Maybe James had been kidnapped ... no, who'd want him? Maybe World War Three had started ...

"... and I urge you to sell as many raffle tickets as possible." Mr. Purcell droned on. "... tour ... stage band ... six hundred dollars short ..." Minerva only half listened. Mr. Purcell was the new principal, and he made everybody nervous, including the teachers. He was small and pale and fussy, and he crept through the halls like a secret agent. And he was really into saving money. Minerva had seen him picking paper-clips out of empty lockers and turning off the lights in the gym even when people were still there.

Everybody wanted Mrs. Sinclair, the super grade eight teacher who had been acting principal last year, to get the job. Especially the kids. But nobody asked the kids, Minerva thought. Hope I get Sinclair next year. If there is a next year. If I don't pull up my gym mark, and my music mark, and my socials mark, I'll be sitting right here listening to poor Mr. Guthrie forget things.

She sighed and flipped open her math book, even though she'd already done enough work for the whole term. A lot of kids groaned about math, and sometimes she did, too, just to be part of the gang. But she really loved it. Every time she worked out a problem, step by step by step, one set of numbers opening to the next and then to the next, she felt powerful and happy and somehow more certain, in command of something bigger than herself. And then finally to write the answer, to sit back and admire the staircase of logic she had climbed, never failed to fascinate and delight her. With numbers she felt at home.

She supposed she got it from her mom. It had amazed her, for as long as she could remember, to watch her mom look at a column of figures and give the total in a couple of seconds. She was a cashier at the big Maple Leaf supermarket over at the plaza, and Minerva had seen her, lots of times, tell a customer what the total was before the register did. Her mother never bragged, but Minerva knew she got a kick out of it.

Mr. Guthrie was saying something, and Minerva tuned back in. ". . .and you may remember the little test at the beginning of...of..." He paused and frowned.

"The week!" someone yelled.

Mr. Guthrie shook his head.

"The month?" asked someone else.

Mr. Guthrie's face cleared and he smiled at them. He had the nicest smile she'd ever seen. The rest of him wasn't much. In fact, he was really kind of ugly in a way. But when he smiled you forgot all about it and smiled right back.

"...the little test to choose students who might profit from a course in computers..." he was saying. Minerva sat up straighter. "...two members of our class...Angelo DeLuz and Minerva Wright...this Thursday..."

Well, all *right*! thought Minerva. Her smile grew broader. Paula Carr, class brain and world champion wimp, turned around and gaped at her in disbelief. All the other kids were staring, too, and suddenly she felt shy. Part of her didn't like the attention: she spent a lot of time trying to be like everybody else, trying not to be noticed. But another part of her loved it. She hadn't been special very often. Except in gym, where she was Minerva the Klutz.

She glanced at Angelo, two aisles over. He'd been in grade six with her last year. She liked him. He never came on all supermacho and phony, like some of the guys. And he was even skinnier than she was, which somehow pleased her, with a narrow brooding face that now was lively with excitement. He turned to look at her and made a quick V sign. She grinned and returned it.

Computers. Wow. She'd tried one during a field trip to the Science Centre, and once when she went looking for James and found him in the arcade at the plaza, she'd played *Defender* a couple of times. But this'd be different. Computers. Real computers. Wow. She could hardly wait till Thursday.

Besides, everybody said that the whole world would soon be run by computers. That if you didn't understand them you'd be left behind. And I'm already behind enough, she thought, as she trudged towards the gym. Just once in my life I'd like to be out in front.

2

SHE spotted Sophie, already changed and reading the Dickens book again. Sophie was good at gym. She was put together better, thought Minerva, with arms and legs the right size for the rest of her. Not like me. Sometimes Minerva had the crazy idea she'd been made from leftovers, from whatever happened to be lying around after everybody else got the good stuff. Next to Sophie she felt all bones and clumsiness. She wondered again why they were friends.

"Hey, Soph! Guess what?"

"Where've you been, Min? Hurry up! Pickle's already taking attendance!"

"Yeah, but guess what, Soph! I got picked..."

"Come on!" Sophie grabbed her arm and pulled her into the gym.

"But I..." began Minerva.

"Tell me later," whispered Sophie.

"Michaloff and Wright, if you've finished your conversation, may we start the class?"

The two girls broke off and stood apart. Minerva made her face go smooth and then hid her real self behind it, like a turtle pulling into its shell. It was the safest way to get through the next hour, and she'd long since perfected the trick. What people saw, what they thought was Minerva, was only the fast-talking, tough, clowning-around Minerva, the fake Minerva, while the real one watched from a secret place.

"Wright, why are you in street clothes?"

Minerva remembered a book on the paperback shelf in the library and murmured, "The cat ate my gymsuit."

Sophie and the girl next to her snuffled with laughter.

"Speak up, Wright! What's your excuse this time?"

"I...I said I have my new swimsuit, Miss Dill. I thought today was swimming."

"You're wrong, Wright." Miss Dill's mouth writhed as she realized she'd made a joke. "Again." She wrote in her notebook. Probably minus five, thought Minerva. More marks lopped off her term average. She sighed and got down on the floor with the others.

Sit-ups. With Pickle snapping off the numbers as if she were counting lashes. After eleven Minerva's stomach muscles screamed at her to surrender. She didn't argue. She stayed still, hoping Pickle wouldn't notice. Wonder what's next, she thought. Maybe ten minutes of hanging by our thumbs.

No. Toe touching. Which was all very well for people who had toes within reach. Minerva didn't. Her legs were long, had grown longer over the summer. She got her fingers down by her knees and waved at her running shoes, then felt a hand in the middle of her back. Pickle.

"Not knees, Wright! Toes! They're at the end of your feet, remember?"

Miss Dill moved on, and Minerva heard someone snicker behind her. "Stick it in your ear," she whispered. Sweat rolled into her eyes and stung. For a moment it felt like tears. She blinked and shook her head impatiently. Her legs trembled, and the backs of her knees burned with strain.

"Outside, girls! Two laps!"

Minerva groaned inwardly. And now, just for a change of pace, folks, we'll zip around the track a couple of times. Easy. Nothing to it. Who does she think I am, Angella Taylor? Not me. Just you watch.

She started off slowly, cautiously. Her jeans felt heavy, like damp tubes of cardboard squeezing her legs. Left, right, left, right, left... Her North Stars crunched on the track's sparse gravel. Far ahead, far, far ahead, she could see Pickle loping along in the lead with the class strung out obediently behind her. Minerva thought of a herd of sheep being led to slaughter.

Left, right, left... Her breath pushed out of her mouth in hot bursts. Her side began to ache. Her tongue felt like the bark of a tree, and she was absolutely certain there was a blister on her left heel. She could see it in her mind, all pink and bloody at first, then, as it puffed up from her flesh, paling to a watery yellow bubble that grew and grew and grew, till it covered her foot, till it crept up her leg to swallow her body, her head, her eyes and nose and mouth...

Pickle shot past on the right and frowned at her. Good grief, she'd already run all the way around the stupid track! thought Minerva and grimly slogged on. Why am I doing this? she asked herself. Isn't there a law against child abuse? Here I am, about to be eaten by a giant blister...

Sophie ran by and threw her a sympathetic grin. Minerva waved, grinned back, and then tripped over her own shoelace. She stumbled and fell, and the gravel bit into her hands and arms. She heard laughing all around her, and someone — probably that airhead Pat Leach — called out, "Hey, Minerva! You heard from your brain lately?"

Rage swept through her, and she scrambled to her feet, ready to fight. But they were far away now, down the track, and she stood there alone and feeling foolish. The anger drained away inside her somewhere, leaving her mouth dry and sour.

Bunch of stupid jocks, she thought. Bet they wouldn't know a computer from a coffee pot. She shrugged and limped off the field into the school. The heck with it. So I fail gym. Big deal. It's not the end of the world. She slumped down behind a pile of mats and let her mind drift back to math class. Only two kids picked, she thought. And one of them was me, Minerva Wright! She grinned.

The lights went out. She straightened up in time to catch a glimpse of Mr. Purcell's grey suit as it vanished into the hall. What a loony! Trying to save a nickel on the hydro bill again. But then Pinevale was crawling with loonies, she thought. Purcell and Dill for sure. Guthrie sometimes. Half the students were space cadets. And even Walter the janitor was a bit weird. He was hooked on the soaps, and every afternoon he disappeared into the furnace room as soon as *Days of Our Lives* came on. And he wouldn't come out, even for fire drill. Nut City, that's what it was.

She ran across the room and turned the lights back on just as the class began to straggle in. Miss Dill ranged behind them like a cranky sheepdog, then stopped and ran in place for a minute. Minerva mingled with the others, pretending to be out of breath. Which wasn't too hard. Finally, Pickle counted them all, to make sure nobody had skipped, and blew her silver whistle.

"Class dismissed!"

Sophie changed, and they jostled their way out to the hall.

"As I was saying before I was so rudely interrupted," said Minerva, "I got picked for the special computer course! How about that, Soph?"

"That's good?"

"Of course it's good!"

"Oh. Well, good, then."

Minerva looked at her, annoyed. "Don't faint with joy over it, Soph."

Sophie laughed. "Sorry, Min. It's just that if I got picked for a computer course, I'd choose a quick death in front of a firing squad."

Minerva stared at her as if she'd suddenly grown another head. How could anyone not like computers? For an instant Sophie seemed like a stranger.

"I'm not surprised, though, Min," she continued. "You're such a brain in that stuff."

"Keep talkin', keep talkin', I love it, don't stop."

They both laughed, and it was all right again.

"It's kind of an honour, I guess," said Minerva, trying to keep her voice casual. "Just two from the whole class get to go, me and Angelo DeLuz — you know that skinny dude who lives near you? And some kids from eight and nine. We start Thursday after school."

"Thursday?"

"Yep."

"This Thursday?"

"Yeah. So?"

"Minerva, you promised to help me sell raffle tickets over at the plaza on Thursday."

Minerva slapped her forehead in dismay. "Aaargh! Oh, Soph, I forgot!" She was silent a moment. "Can we do it another day?"

Sophie turned to face her, her glance level and unsmiling. "No. All the money has to be turned in at the end of the week, and I've got band rehearsals the other days." She stopped. Minerva couldn't think of anything to say.

"Are you going to come or not?" Sophie asked finally.

Minerva pushed her fingers through her hair in a quick worried way. "Well, gee, Soph, it's the first class! I don't think I should miss..."

Sophie interrupted. "You can miss it, Min! You're smart enough to miss one lesson, aren't you? Besides, you promised!"

"Yeah, I know, Soph, but..."

"I mean, this is important! If we don't sell enough tickets, then the whole Quebec tour is off. And it took me a month to talk my dad into letting me go! You know how I hate asking people for money, and I was really counting on you..." Her voice trailed off, and she looked away.

Minerva stared down the hall without seeing anything. She felt bad about breaking the promise. But she had to. She turned to Sophie. "Soph, this is just as important to me, maybe more, don't you see that? It's different for you, you're so terrific at everything. You get prizes and pull off nineties and play clarinet and sax in the band. I get zilch, I barely pass, and I bet I'm the only person in the school who can't even hum right! This is probably my one chance to be good at something, and I don't want to mess up!" Minerva's voice had risen, and three girls from grade eight looked around and laughed. Minerva glared at them.

"I mean, how'd you like to be the school klutz? It's not all that great a career, you know." She felt herself trembling and leaned against the wall. "Soph, give me a break, eh?"

"Okay, okay, okay." Sophie was looking at her oddly. "Let's forget it."

Both of them stared at the floor, then at each other.

"I don't want us to have a fight, Soph."

"Me neither." Sophie smiled as if she were trying it on for size.

Minerva grinned in relief. "Hey, Soph, you want to go to that new De Niro flick on Saturday? He's your main man, right?"

"It's restricted, isn't it?"

"Naw, adult accompaniment. They always let me in, and I'll tell them you're my little sister."

They laughed.

"Anyway, Soph, I'll see you at lunch for sure."

"No, you won't, you'll see me in an hour for family studies. With your friend and mine, Miss Dill."

"Is that today? I forgot!" Minerva looked stricken. "Did we have homework?"

Sophie started to laugh again. "Relax, kid! We're up to how babies are made. She wouldn't dare give us homework in that!"

"Bet it's more fun than sewing," said Minerva. She saw Purcell heading towards them and looked at her watch. "We better split or we'll get arrested for loitering. See ya, Soph."

She touched Sophie's arm briefly and ducked into her homeroom.

3

DARN. Where was he?

Minerva scowled at the thinning parade of little kids trickling out of James's school. It was twenty to four already and no sign of him. Where *was* he?

Rotten kid, she thought. Why do I have to look after him anyway? When I was nine nobody looked after me. I looked after myself. Mom and Dad worry about him too much. She grinned. If they knew the truth they'd lock him up.

She remembered again the crowded, noisy, happy years downtown, when there'd always been a cousin or an aunt to watchdog James, and all her time had been her own to do with as she wished. The neighbourhood was friendly, familiar, old, hers; she'd known every house, every corner store, every street; each crack in the sidewalks, each tree in the tiny park a block away had belonged to her. Then — *zap!* The

"FOR SALE" sign went up one day, the "SOLD" sign the next, the wreckers arrived the day after that, and in no time they'd moved way out here where everything was strange and new. Where the only stores were in shopping malls and there weren't any sidewalks at all. Where the parks were too big and the trees were too small.

She sighed. Well, at least she had her own bedroom now. And then there was Sophie. And now a chance at computers. Her mind leaped ahead to Thursday, and she only gradually became aware that a small boy was gazing up at her.

"You James Wright's sister?" the boy asked.

"I confess! I confess! Don't hit me again!" answered Minerva.

The boy continued to gaze at her, his face stolid. Finally he said, "He's gone," and started to turn away.

Minerva grabbed the back of his jacket and hauled him closer. "Gone where?"

Again the blank stare. What's with this kid? thought Minerva. They forget to put in new batteries this morning?

The boy jerked his head south. "Plaza," he said.

Minerva relaxed her grip. "Oh, shoot!" she muttered. Now she'd have to find him. He wasn't supposed to hang out over there. Especially after school. Or by himself. She hurried her pace. Now we'll miss the ten-to-four bus. And the ten-after. And we haven't done the breakfast dishes. Shoot!

She turned into the plaza and passed under the huge sign that said, "Fifty-two stores for your shopping pleasure." Which one was he in? Of course. The arcade. She dodged through the crowds and ran up the escalator to Level Two, then down the wide hall to The Gamekeeper's, stopping for a second inside the door until her eyes adjusted to the dimness. The only light, bluish and flickering, came from half a dozen screens along one wall of the gallery-like room. She glanced around. No James. Some kids his size were playing *Baby Pac-Man* and *Food Fight*, and noisy cheers went up as Zorba the chef got a watermelon in the face. *Donkey Kong* sat dark and forlorn in a corner — everybody was tired of it. A man in a suit and tie hunched over the battered frame of *Mad Planets*, clutching at the joystick and looking grumpy. But most of the kids were huddled around a game near the back of the store. Minerva walked towards them.

"Hi, Minerva!"

She heard the jingle of coins and turned to see Angelo DeLuz smiling at her. Tied around his waist was a wide-pocketed black apron. "Need some change?" he asked, and the blue light glinted on the pile of quarters in his outstretched hand.

She smiled back at him, glad to see a familiar face. "You work here, Angelo?"

"Yup. Just started. A couple of afternoons a week and Saturdays if Mr. Mellors needs me. A lot easier than my paper route. More money, too!" He let the coins cascade from one hand to the other.

"Sounds neat. Hey, have you seen my brother around? He's escaped custody again."

"He's probably at the back with everybody else." He pointed to the crowd. "New game in, *Challenge of the Jedi*. Supposed to be hard. People are really tripping on it."

They moved closer. Minerva caught sight of the new girl, her spiky pink hair startling in the gloom. A gold hoop earring, so big it grazed her shoulder, swung from her left ear, and she wore Mark Hofmann's black leather jacket like a prize she'd won in battle. Maybe she had, thought Minerva. Nearby was Patricia Leach, and her eyes were narrow and furious as she looked at the new girl and then at Mark, who was leaning over the game like Dracula drinking blood. His thick blond hair was in tight curls all over his head, and the muscles in his arms bulged and gleamed. Good looking, if you liked the animal type, thought Minerva. But not too swift. And not worth fighting over, for sure.

A sigh arose from the crowd as Mark lasered a mutant invader, and then a groan when two of his robot ships flared and vanished. The next wave of attackers burst onto the screen and zoomed in from the ten o'clock position. Lights flashed. Beeps beeped. Red arrows of energy and bolts of blue flame leaped at the onlookers as Mark shoved the joystick here, there, back, forward, his thumb hugging the button. He launched his third fleet of fighters, and they swarmed

22

out of the blackness like killer bees, their only goal to protect the mothership.

The crowd sighed again, then drew in its breath as four fighters blew apart in a blazing shower. Minerva stared as if hypnotized at the tiny drama of fake death unfolding in front of her. Mark's squadron downed one, two, five, seven of the invaders — but three rocketed through the fiery grid towards the unguarded right flank of the mothership. Mark yanked at the stick, his body swaying like a boxer's, and sweat glistened on his upper lip. He jockeyed what remained of his shattered escort into tight formation below the three mutants and prepared to blast them out of the galaxy. He waited as they drew within range, and the crowd waited with him. The score flashed at the top of the screen: 12,500,000 — 50,000 points from a new record. An alien swooped low; Mark's thumb moved; the alien was no more. A second attacker hurtled in from the left and exploded into orange stars. The score flashed once, twice: 10,000 points short of the record. A hush settled on the room. The third and last invader hung in the void for a split second, then launched itself at the brooding mothership. Mark tensed, leaned forward — and the screen went dark.

A huge groan arose, and cries of "Tough!" and "Great game, Mark!" were heard. Applause spattered like sudden rain. The girl wearing Mark's jacket flung an arm around his middle in sympathy. Patricia Leach smiled, and Minerva thought of *Jaws*.

For a moment Mark's hands hung loose like bunches

of bananas, then curled into large fists. He smashed one of them into the screen. It stayed dark.

"Who did it?" he yelled. He reached behind the game and held up the loose electrical cord. "Which one of you turkeys pulled the plug? I'll kill him!" His big head sank into his neck as he moved forward. The crowd fell back.

Then Minerva saw James crouched down behind the game, his eyes white and scared. She squirmed through the press of bodies until she stood beside him and held out her hand.

"I'll kill him!" Mark roared again.

Minerva looked around for the nearest door. Abruptly, Angelo appeared out of the shadows and whispered, "Back way. Come on!"

Minerva followed him, tripping over cables, creeping past *Donkey Kong*, *Vampire*, and *Millipede*, with James scrambling after her on all fours. She heard Mark shouting again, and then Pat Leach's wispy voice saying, "I saw a little black kid back there!"

Rotten fink, thought Minerva. She glanced over her shoulder. Mark had wheeled around and was bulling his way towards them. In the strange half-light he seemed to glow like The Incredible Hulk. Frantic, she looked ahead. Angelo braced the door open with one arm, waved them on with the other. Minerva scooped up James and ran.

Pickle should see me now, she thought. Nothing like a murder threat to improve your speed. She zigzagged through the shoppers in front of Eaton's and darted across the parking lot to the bus stop, then set James firmly on his feet.

"One of these days, James..." she began.

"I didn't mean to, Min! Honest!"

"Fine, I'll carve that on your gravestone."

James stared up at her, then squeaked, "You...you think he'll really kill me, Minnie?"

Minerva kept her face straight and said, "Not right away. He'll probably break your arms and legs first." She watched James blink in terror. The bus drew up, and they climbed on. "And don't call me Minnie or I'll kill you before Hofmann does!" She shoved him into an empty seat, glared at him, and walked back to stand near the rear door. She laid her cheek against the cool steel of the upright and sighed.

And so, folks, she announced silently, we come to the end of an average day in the life of Minerva Wright. A race riot in the lobby, a fight with her best friend, a disaster in gym, and a mad killer loose in the plaza... Tune in tomorrow for more exciting adventures...

She looked at her watch and groaned. Five-thirty. Just to round out the day they'd be late...

Minerva put the carton of three-flavour ice cream she'd just bought behind her back. She opened the door and they stepped quietly into the apartment. Maybe nobody was home yet...

No such luck. On the big armchair beside the TV lay

her father's jacket, walkie-talkie, and cap, its silver hospital badge touched with the sunlight slanting through the balcony doors. Then her mother came in from the kitchen, still in her supermarket uniform. And drying her hands on a tea towel. Not good, thought Minerva.

"Minerva, where have you been?"

"Oh hi, Mom. Didn't think you'd be home yet."

"Apparently."

Minerva glanced at her mother. Oh-oh. No smile. She looked at James. His face wore a pleading expression, and his lips formed the words, "Don't tell."

"I...uh...I had a special project to do, sorry to be late, shall I do the dishes?" said Minerva in a rush.

"They're done."

"Oh. Guess I'll peel the potatoes then."

"Dad's making supper."

"Oh." Well, she said to herself, I'll just go drown myself in the toilet bowl, okay? Aloud she said, "James and I will set the table." She smiled menacingly at her brother. "Right, James?"

"Right, Min."

They walked into the kitchen and Minerva slipped the ice cream into the freezer. Their father was peering into the oven. Minerva sniffed. "Hi, Dad. Smells good in here. What's cookin'?"

Greg Wright unbent his long frame and took off his oven mitts with a flourish. "Dinner fit for royalty tonight, you lucky people. Baked lake trout with cayenne sauce." He smiled down at them. He was very tall, and Minerva sometimes had a terrifying premonition that she would grow to the same height.

"Is that fish?" asked James.

Minerva threw him a warning look. He hated fish. She wasn't all that crazy about it herself, but this was hardly the time to say so. "Sounds terrific, Dad," she lied. He was a security guard at Oxbridge County Hospital but he was learning to be a cook, and ever since he'd started his chef course over at the college they'd had weird stuff for supper. Some of it even tasted pretty good.

She picked up the knives, forks, and spoons and went into the little dining alcove. Her mother was in the living room half asleep, with her shoes off and her feet tucked under her. Even when she's tired she looks great, Minerva thought. Her mother was small and tidy, with terrific eyes and cheekbones, her skin rich and golden in the afternoon light. She never tripped or ran into things, and when she moved it was like watching music.

Minerva sighed and glanced at the gold-framed photograph on the TV set, the one of her father and mother and herself when she was four. She still remembered that day. They'd been at the beach, with the sun hot and white in the middle of the sky, and her father had called to her. She had run to where he stood, tall as a tree it seemed then, and he had swept her up to the place he kept for her on one warm shoulder. And she had looked out from that great height and seen farther than she'd ever seen.

The resemblance was so clear it was almost funny: there she was, on his shoulder, long, skinny and sharp-cornered, a smaller twin of him. Every time they saw her the cousins and aunts told the same story, of how, when she was born, they had taken one look and said, "She's the dead spittin' image of Gregory Edward!" Which really grossed her out. Not that her father wasn't a neat guy — but sometimes she wished she could have taken after her mother instead.

James came in carrying the plates and cups and spread them here and there on the table as if he were dealing cards, then padded into the living room to stand by his mother's chair.

"You asleep, Mom?"

No answer.

James picked up his father's walkie-talkie and spoke into it. "Calling mothership, calling mothership, come in please, need to make emergency landing, over..."

Minerva saw her mother's mouth curve upwards briefly and one eye open. "Cleared for landing, come in on usual runway, over..."

James laughed and jumped into her lap, and her arms closed around him in a hug. Minerva took a couple of steps towards them, then stopped. Just for a second she had wanted to be sitting there, too. She smiled. She'd look like a stork on a sparrow's nest.

Her father poked his head through the doorway. "Vicky, we don't have any lemons!" Then he saw James with the walkie-talkie and frowned. "I told you not to fool with that, son."

Minerva listened. James might get heck. Good.

"You want to play with walkie-talkies, go play with your own," her father was saying.

"Mine are just toys," answered James.

"So? They work."

James looked carefully at his father, then shook his head. "Not any more. Antenna's busted off one."

Oh boy. Now he'll really get it. Minerva put her hand up to hide a smile.

"Greg, there's a lemon on the fridge door beside the eggs," said Victoria Wright.

Darn! Good ol' Mom comes to the rescue, thought Minerva. As usual.

"Oh," said her father. His head disappeared into the kitchen, then popped out again. "James, show it to me after supper. Maybe I can fix it."

He would, too, Minerva thought as she put the milk and sugar on the table. He could fix just about anything: stopped clocks, windows that stuck, chairs with shaky legs, toasters that only toasted one side, and all the toys she and James had broken over the years. She remembered a tricycle she'd left out on the sidewalk on St. Clair. A florist's van had hit it, and the rear wheels were bent, the spokes broken or twisted or gone. She had taken it to her father and said, "Daddy fix." And he had. Almost as good as new. "Daddy fix." It was almost a family joke now: whenever anything went wrong, all of them, sometimes even her father, said it. "Daddy fix." "Daddy fix."

She surveyed the table, then went back to the kitchen to get extra spoons for the ice cream. Her special surprise dessert. She'd bring it out and then tell them about the computer course. She rubbed the spoons on her T-shirt till they gleamed as if lit from inside.

Her father appeared at the doorway. In his fake butler's voice he said, "Ladies and gentlemen, dinner is served." They sat down and he put a big platter on the table. Minerva looked at it and swallowed hard. On it, like a dead body on a slab, lay the whole fish. She could see its tail and its fins and worst of all its head, with blind milky eyes popping out of it. She glanced at James. His eyes were like the fish's and his mouth had fallen open. She stared at the fish once more. Around it were slices of lemon, pale rings of onion, chunks of carrot and potato, and some green weedy things. Looks like it died in a garbage dump, she thought. She swallowed again.

"Greg, that's real nice!" said Victoria.

"Yeah, it's fabulous, Dad. A masterpiece," said Minerva. She kicked James under the table.

"Yeah, sure is," he mumbled.

Their father beamed and began to serve it up. "The recipe says you should take the eyes out and put maraschino cherries in the sockets..."

Minerva felt her stomach flutter in alarm. She took her plate from him and tried to go deaf.

"...but we didn't have any cherries," her father went on. He stuck the big fork under one eye and flipped it out on the platter. "You know, the eyes are a real delicacy. Who wants one?"

"To *eat*?" James looked at his father in horror.

Minerva saw her father's mouth twitch suspiciously. She called his bluff. "*You* eat them, Dad. After all, you cooked the fish." She stared at him. He stared back and started to grin. Slowly he reached forward, picked up an eye between his thumb and forefinger, and moved it towards his mouth. Minerva watched in growing disbelief. Just as he opened his mouth, her nerve failed and she turned her head away.

"Mmmm," said her father. "Delicious!"

He'd fooled her again, she knew. It was probably in his shirt pocket. She took a bite of the fish. It wasn't too bad.

James slid out of his chair without a sound. His mother glanced up. "Where you going, James?"

"I just wanna catch the last of *Spiderman*," he answered. He took his plate with him into the living room.

Coward! thought Minerva. Bet he sneaks into the kitchen and gets a peanut butter sandwich. She ate her dinner fast and hurried to the fridge. Quickly she spooned big helpings of ice cream into the good glass fruit bowls and carried them back to the table, smiling.

Her mother raised her eyebrows. "How come the ice cream, Min?"

"Because we're celebrating!"

"Oh?" said her mother. "What? You getting out of doing the dishes?"

Minerva's smile vanished. Thanks a lot, Mom, she thought. She swallowed some ice cream without tasting it. "No, me getting picked to take a computer course at school." She looked at them and waited.

"Really!" said her mother.

"Yeah?" said her father.

"Seems like it's the coming thing," said her mother.

"They got 'em all over the hospital now," said her father.

"They're talking about computerizing the cash at the store," said her mother. "That should mess things up."

Her father laughed. "Remember when we got the hydro bill for fifteen hundred dollars?"

Then her mother laughed. "Seems every time I go into the bank, the tellers say, 'The machines are down.'" She shook her head. "Can't see that they help much."

Minerva stared at them, angry and bewildered. "It's…it's a special thing, you know!" Her voice was louder than she meant it to be. "Only a few kids were picked. And I'm one of them!" Why didn't they understand?

Then the telephone rang, and her mother got up to answer it and said in a hurry, "Well, that's good, Min, but don't let it interfere, you've got plenty to do already…hello?"

And then James came in and said "Daddy fix" in his cute disgusting way, and dumped his walkie-talkies and the loose antenna on the table. And whatever her father had been going to say wasn't said at all.

Minerva stared at her ice cream. It was melting. She

pushed her spoon around in it until the pink and the brown and the creamy white were all mixed together. It looked like mud.

Later, as she cleared the table, her father looked up from his soldering iron. "They think you're good at the school, Min?"

She nodded.

"Maybe you'll be a big success, be your own boss some day, like Uncle Clifford back home, eh?"

"Maybe."

He smiled at her. "I'm glad, Minerva."

It wasn't enough, but it was something.

4

IT wasn't like school at all, thought Minerva. The room didn't even look like a classroom. For one thing the chairs — eight of them, ranged in two rows of four — had cushions. In front of each chair was a small table with a keyboard and a little TV screen on top of a black box. Against the far wall was a long wide desk. Half of it was empty; on the other half she saw four screens and keyboards, with cables and cords curling out of them like tails, and a couple of machines whose toothed rollers held paper fed from a carton on the floor below. Printers, she guessed.

Mrs. Sinclair and Mr. Guthrie were there, and lounging in one of the chairs was a young man wearing thick glasses and eating potato chips. And next to him, Minerva noticed in surprise, was Mark Hofmann's punk girl friend. Then Mr. Purcell came in, and all the kids hurried to find a place.

He cleared his throat. "Good afternoon," he said. "You have been chosen to participate in Pinevale's first computer class. This is a privilege, and it carries with it considerable responsibility. The machines in front of you, generously provided by the Board — at my request, I might add — cost a great deal of money. I expect you to treat them with care. They are not toys." He looked around the room and frowned. "Mrs. Sinclair and Mr. Guthrie are here to supervise you for today, but the major teaching burden will fall to Mr. Richard Campbell, a computer science student of some brilliance."

"Thanks, Uncle Pete," said the young man eating potato chips.

Uncle? thought Minerva. Probably hired him cheap.

Mr. Purcell frowned at his nephew, then again at the class. "I trust you will behave as mature individuals." He didn't look as if he trusted them with anything. "Good afternoon."

Everybody relaxed after he left. Minerva stealthily let her fingers play on the keys and glanced at Angelo beside her. He was doing the same thing. They grinned at each other.

Mrs. Sinclair was talking. "...so remember, always remember, that the computer is only a machine. It's not magic and it can't think. Compared to you, the computer is about as smart as a worm. It's a machine that stores, arranges, and manipulates information — after you tell it how. It's as if you had an extra brain to do the simple boring jobs like arithmetic and filing. It's not nearly as complicated or clever as the brain inside your head. But it's many times faster. It's an encyclopedia, a filing cabinet, and a calculator all rolled into one. It's your personal information slave."

"Like R2D2," said a boy.

She smiled and shook her head. "Not nearly as smart. Some day we'll have AIMS — Artificial Intelligence Machines — like R2 and C-3PO. Scientists are working on them now, but they're years away." She paused, then said, "Perhaps one of you will help invent the first R2D2.

There was a murmuring sigh after that, and then a silence. Minerva felt a shiver run through her. Once again her fingers caressed the keys.

"I know you want to get started," said Mrs. Sinclair. "So it's time for Mr. Campbell to take over." She nodded at Mr. Purcell's nephew.

"Hi," he said. "First, I'd like you to call me Rick. I'm not all that much older than you. Second, I'm not going to do much teaching, because you'll be teaching yourselves most of the time. I'm just here to help. So if you get fouled up or you can't figure something out, just yell 'Rick!'" He crumpled up the potato chip bag and stuffed it in his pocket. "Third, you know my name but I don't know yours. Suppose you tell me."

They went down the rows then, saying their names. Of the eight, Minerva knew only Angelo. The punk girl's name was Barbara Fairfax. Her voice was low and pleasant.

"Never figured her for a computer course," Minerva whispered to Angelo.

"More like Elementary Weird," he whispered back. "Or Advanced Illegal Substances."

Minerva chuckled and glanced again at Barbara Fairfax. Wild make-up. Crazy pink hair. And that one huge earring, big as a saucer. But a good face underneath it all, with a mouth that looked ready to laugh and thoughtful blue eyes. Minerva was suddenly sure that the punk stuff was just a disguise, something for the real Barbara to hide behind. Maybe she had a secret place, too, and didn't want anyone to know about it.

Rick was talking again. "... so we'll start out on the little microcomputers in front of you, using what's called simplified BASIC. That's a special language for computers, and it's stored on a disk inside the disk drive." He pointed to the black box underneath Angelo's screen. "BASIC's easy, and you'll learn it fast. Once you do, you can move up to more complex programming using extended BASIC, on the machines over there." He gestured towards the long desk by the wall. "Those are terminals hooked up to the big computer at the Board of Education, called a mainframe. At that point you'll have to make up a password for yourself, which is a kind of key that unlocks the door to the mainframe and its data bank."

Rick stopped for breath, squinted at them through his glasses, then took the glasses off and cleaned them on his tie. Minerva hoped she didn't look as stupid as she felt. All the strange new words were tumbling around in her head.

"Okay. That's enough talk for now. Let's have some fun. Open that little booklet beside your machine — and power up!"

"Press the orange switch at the rear of the cabinet," Minerva read. She did. There was a brief buzzing sound, like an angry bee, and a small red light glowed on the black box. The word READY appeared in the upper left corner of the screen, and underneath it a little square blinked at her. She blinked back, then looked at the pamphlet beside her. The little square was called a cursor. Slowly at first, with halting and uncertain fingers, Minerva went through page one, page two, page three. She sent the cursor skidding up and down the screen; as quick as light she multiplied and divided enormous numbers; she put words in; she took words out; she filled the screen, then emptied it with a touch. And with each move her mind seemed sharper, her fingers surer, her pleasure keener.

She turned the page. "You are now ready to write a program. Type the following, inserting your own name at Line 30. YOU MUST ENCLOSE YOUR STATE-MENT IN QUOTES TO CARRY OUT THE PRINT COM-MAND." She began to type, and when she was finished the screen said:

```
10 PRINT "      EGO TRIP
20 PRINT
```

```
30 PRINT "MINERVA WRIGHT IS GOOD-LOOKING
          AND CLEVER"

40 GOTO 30
```

Then in the notes she read, "To run your program, type
RUN and press the RETURN key." Minerva did as she
was told. The screen flashed.

```
SYNTAX ERROR LINE 10
```

She frowned in disappointment. What error?
Quickly she typed LIST and her program appeared
once more. She stared at Line 10. Ha! No quotes after
TRIP. She put them in, typed RUN, hit RETURN, and
saw:

```
              EGO TRIP

MINERVA WRIGHT IS GOOD-LOOKING AND CLEVER

MINERVA WRIGHT IS GOOD-LOOKING AND CLEVER

MINERVA WRIGHT IS GOOD-LOOKING AND CLEVER

MINERVA WRIGHT IS GOOD-LOOKING AND CLEVER
```

The screen filled with the sentence, over and over and
over, almost faster than her eye could follow, scrolling
upwards to make ever more room to print and print
and print again that one shining hypnotic message:

```
MINERVA WRIGHT IS GOOD-LOOKING AND CLEVER

MINERVA WRIGHT IS GOOD-LOOKING AND CLEVER
```

On and on it went, repeating and repeating, until Minerva could almost believe it was true. It would go on forever unless she stopped it, the booklet said. She grinned. Why should I? I never had so many compliments in my life! What an amazing machine! It knew the truth about her right away! She laughed out loud and turned again to the notes. "This is called an INFINITE LOOP," she read. An infinite loop. An infinite loop. She said the words over and over in her mind as if they were a chant. They sounded mysterious to her, and grand, and full of echoes from a place she knew yet didn't know. "I have made an infinite loop," she murmured, and then glanced around quickly. Nobody had heard. Nobody was listening. Angelo, beside her, seemed under a spell; Barbara gazed at her screen in concentration; Rick was hunched over a terminal talking to himself.

She hit the BREAK key. The machine obeyed instantly, and Minerva felt a tiny surge of power run through her, as if her blood had trembled. She stared at the screen.

```
MINERVA WRIGHT IS GOOD-LOOKING AND CLEVER

MINERVA WRIGHT IS GOOD-LOOKING AND CLEVER

BREAK AT LINE 30
```

She had the sudden odd feeling that the computer approved of her. As if it had looked up and smiled, just like her dad the other day. Without wanting anything in return. Sometimes she knew, she just *knew*, that people were nice to her or said nice things because they wanted something. They wanted her to be quiet, or to go away, or to do them some kind of favour. It was as if they were bribing her with fake money, and it made her feel small and unimportant and cheated. She wasn't sure just when she'd started to notice this, but now if people — even Sophie — paid her a compliment she often wondered if they really meant it. Or what they wanted.

But the computer — this terrific machine sitting in front of her — wasn't phony like that at all. When it said "MINERVA WRIGHT IS GOOD-LOOKING AND CLEVER" it didn't want anything, didn't expect anything. It didn't cheat, and it didn't turn away. To it, right now, she was the most important person in the world, the only person in the world.

She shook her head. What was she thinking of? The computer was just a machine. Mrs. Sinclair had said that at least three times. It just sat there and did what she told it to do. It couldn't approve or disapprove of her. It didn't care. And yet, she thought, it seemed to.

READY, said the screen. The cursor winked.

She turned to the next exercise. It looked long and complicated. "A Conversation With Your Computer." Why not? We're already friends, she thought. "How to use INPUT, DIM, $, and; in programming." She did the short examples first, checking the screen against the booklet again and again. Then she put it all together, and it read:

```
10 REM PROGRAM ALADDIN WRITTEN BY MINERVA

20 DIM REPLY$(4)

30 REPLY$(1) = "WHAT IS YOUR NAME?"

40 REPLY$(2) = "HELLO "

50 REPLY$(3) = "HOW ARE YOU TODAY?"

60 REPLY$(4) = "I AM READY TO OBEY YOU, "

70 PRINT REPLY$(1)

80 INPUT NAME$

90 PRINT REPLY$(2);NAME$

100 INPUT A$

110 PRINT REPLY$(3)

120 INPUT A$

130 PRINT REPLY$(4);NAME$

140 STOP
```

Minerva sat back and looked at it. Then she held her breath and typed the command RUN. The screen flashed. At each prompting question mark she responded.

```
WHAT IS YOUR NAME?

? MINERVA

HELLO MINERVA

? HI FRIEND

HOW ARE YOU TODAY?

? I AM READY TO TAKE COMMAND.  HOW ARE
  YOU?

I AM READY TO OBEY YOU, MINERVA

BREAK AT LINE 140
```

Minerva felt a jolt of pleasure, and again that sense of
power flicked her mind like an invisible whip. Wow.
What a rush! she thought. Where have you been all my
life? She stared at that final bright line, that oath of
loyalty. I AM READY TO OBEY YOU, MINERVA. I
AM READY TO OBEY YOU, MINERVA.   No wonder
the program was called ALADDIN.

She sighed with satisfaction and leaned back. There
was a cramp in her neck. She rubbed at it and looked
around.

The room was almost empty.

Angelo sat beside her, still as stone, fingers curved
over the keyboard and eyes fixed on the screen. Rick
was at his terminal. She could hear his soft mumble
punctuated by the rapidfire stutter of typing. Both of
them looked spaced-out, thought Minerva, and then

realized that only minutes ago she must have looked like that, too.

Everyone else was gone. She peered at her watch. Ten after five? It couldn't be! She'd told James she'd meet him at the bus stop at five. She got up fast and pushed her chair back.

Rick turned around and smiled fuzzily, as if he'd just awakened. "Going now, Minerva?"

She was pleased he'd remembered her name. "Yes, I'm late already, sir."

He shook his head. "I'm not 'sir,' I'm Rick. Remember?"

"Okay, s... Rick."

"If you want to drop in Saturday, I'll be here most of the day."

"Really?" She could feel herself grinning.

"Sure."

"Yeah, well, maybe I'll come for a while."

Angelo stirred, stretched, stood up. "Hey, Minerva, wait a sec. I'm coming, too."

They were silent as they hurried from the school. Minerva still couldn't believe a whole hour had gone by without her knowing it. It had felt like about five minutes! And she hadn't even heard the others leave. It was as if she'd been all alone in the room. No, not quite alone, she thought. The computer was there. What a trip! She'd been right out of herself. She hadn't felt like that since she was a kid, before she knew about the two Minervas inside her, one acting the way people seemed to expect, and the other safe and hidden. For the past hour there had been only one Minerva. Both parts of her now felt joined together, and together they seemed to make a bigger person, a surer person, a person she liked better. For the first time in her life she felt she knew where she was going. She'd probably get heck for being late, but somehow it didn't bother her. It couldn't spoil, couldn't even touch, the sweetness of what had happened. She could hardly wait till Saturday.

Angelo murmured something beside her.

"What'd you say, Angelo?" She saw James at the bus stop and waved.

"I said I can hardly wait till Saturday."

She glanced at him. He seemed as changed as she was. They smiled at each other as the bus opened its doors.

5

MINERVA yawned. Then she yawned again. If I had any say, she thought, I'd abolish Monday morning. We'd start the week in the afternoon instead. She clung to the steel post by the door, swaying as the bus lurched through the streets. James had squeezed in behind the driver again, and every now and then his hands curled around an imaginary steering wheel.

She looked down the aisle but the bus was so crowded she couldn't see Sophie. Why were there always more passengers on Mondays? They should organize it better, she thought, put more buses on. Computer would figure it out fast, I bet.

She yawned again. She hadn't had enough sleep. When her mother had called this morning she was sure it was a bad joke. Her own fault, though. She'd stayed awake half the night working on a program, with a flashlight under the covers.

Saturday had been great. She'd raced through the vacuuming and dusting and been at the school by ten o'clock. Rick was there, just as he'd promised. She'd learned a lot, gone on to longer programs, done some IF...THEN statements, tried out a few subroutines. And the time had gone so fast again. She'd worked till almost four, not even hungry. Better watch that, she thought, or I'll be skinnier than ever.

Some people got off at the hospital where her dad worked, and she caught a glimpse of Sophie at the back. She waggled her fingers. There was no response. Guess she didn't see me, thought Minerva.

She could hardly wait to show Angelo the game she was working on. It was a detective game, not nearly as complicated as the arcade games, but still fun. Fun to make up, for sure. Rick had been amazed, then he'd helped her a bit and told her to go ahead. He even said he'd fix it so she could use the computer room whenever she liked. And this week she'd be getting access to the Board's mainframe! She grinned. Now if only I could program my timetable to get out of gym, music, socials and a few other things...

The bus stopped at the school. James dashed past her and out the front door, and she saw Sophie getting off at the back, with her saxophone and the usual stack of books.

"Hey, Soph! Wait up!" she yelled.

Sophie didn't turn. What's with her? thought Minerva. She walked faster and caught up to Sophie just as she reached the doors of the school.

"Hey Soph! Didn't you hear me? Why didn't you wait?"

Sophie looked up at her. She wasn't smiling. "I guess because I did a lot of waiting on Saturday."

"Saturday?" repeated Minerva, puzzled. "Saturday I was here, fooling with the computer."

"Oh?" Sophie started to walk away. "I was standing in line at the Northview Theatre waiting for my friend to show up. She didn't."

Minerva stood still for a moment, groaned, and then caught up to Sophie again. "Oh, Soph!"

Sophie stared at her in silence.

"I'm sorry, Soph! I'm such a jerk! I'm just no good, that's all!"

"I'll go along with that," said Sophie.

"I don't blame you for being mad, Soph."

"Thank you. Very generous of you, I'm sure."

"Maybe you won't believe this, but...but I forgot!"

"Not the first time, as I recall."

Minerva smiled a little. "I think I must have a bubble memory."

"What?"

"It's a term in computers."

"How incredibly fascinating, my dear."

Oh-oh, thought Minerva. I think I bombed. She's starting to talk like a book. Which means she's really upset.

They walked along the corridor in silence. Minerva felt terrible. How could she have forgotten a date with her best friend? Desperate to get Sophie talking, she said, "Hey Soph, you'll never guess who's taking the computer course!"

"If I'll never guess, you'd better tell me."

Minerva looked at her. Still mad. "The punker!"

"The new girl?"

"Yeah! Imagine, huh?"

"You mean the thing attached to Hofmann's body?"

"Yeah, like a big pink wart!"

Sophie smiled, then tried not to.

Minerva felt herself slide into the other part of her, the clown part. She held an imaginary microphone to her mouth and beckoned to some grade six kids who had stopped to watch. "We interrupt this program to bring you a special bulletin! It has just been reported that Sophie Michaloff may have smiled! If this is true, ladies and gentlemen, it could change all our lives, especially Minerva Wright's."

Out of the corner of her eye Minerva saw Sophie start to grin. "Yes, folks, it's true! Sophie Michaloff is smiling! The crowd is going wild! Just listen to that applause!"

All the kids clapped.

"Just listen to those cheers!"

All the kids cheered.

Sophie was laughing now, leaning against the wall. Minerva stepped nearer. "Miss Michaloff, can you tell our radio audience if you're still friends with Minerva Wright?"

Sophie's face grew serious for a moment, then she smiled again. "Yes, it's true. We're friends."

"Really?" asked Minerva.

"Really."

All the kids cheered again. Minerva did, too, then said, "Here, let me carry your sax. It's bigger than you are."

They turned the corner into the music room. Minerva walked to the big storage area at the back and swung the sax case in with the other instruments.

"What's her name, E.T. Two?"

Minerva laughed. "Nope. It's sort of ordinary. Barbara Fairfax. And you know, Soph, I think she's normal underneath."

"You mean normal, as in human?"

Minerva laughed again, but she felt uncomfortable. There was an edge in Sophie's voice she'd never heard before.

"Yeah, I think she's probably just like me or you."

"Last time I looked in a mirror I didn't see a big pink wart, as I recall."

"Aw c'mon, Soph! Lay off her! I meant inside. I think maybe all the make-up and the hair and the weird clothes are a disguise."

"Oh? How can you tell? Besides, you were the one who called her a wart! Make up your mind!" Sophie's voice was almost shrill, and Minerva turned to her in surprise.

"Make up my mind about what? Soph, all I'm saying is that sometimes after you get to know people, they're different than you thought."

"Well, I certainly agree with you there!"

Minerva stared at her. She felt as if she'd just walked into a swamp and if she moved she'd get sucked under. Sophie stared back, and Minerva could almost hear words waiting in the air, waiting to be spoken. Words that would either make the last minutes vanish — or lead them both into a place they'd never get out of. And she didn't know which words to say.

The five-to-nine bell rang, and Minerva almost laughed. At last I know what "saved by the bell" really means, she thought.

The tension snapped. They walked out of the music room and separated at the north corner to go to their homerooms. With her glance averted, Sophie said, "See you at lunch, Min?"

Shoot! thought Minerva. I wanted to check out my game program. Then she heard herself say, "Um, gee, Soph, can't make it today. Got to finish a project for this aft." She made her face go smooth and closed.

"Oh," said Sophie. "Okay, Minerva. I think I understand. See you around." She walked down the hall without looking back.

She doesn't believe me, thought Minerva. And I don't blame her. I don't believe me either. First time I ever lied to her. And she knows I lied. But it's all her fault! Can't she understand how I feel? I never complain about all her silly rehearsals. And she was really mean about Barbara, too! Shoot! If only people were more like computers! A computer never got into fights with you, you never had to be careful what you said to it, you couldn't hurt its feelings and it couldn't hurt yours. You didn't have to be a clown — or a liar — to keep it friendly.

She thought back to her clowning around to make Sophie stop being mad, the many times she'd done that, not just with Sophie but with other people, too, so they'd like her better, and she was sick of herself. Or at least the self that kept doing that kind of thing. With the computer it was different. With the computer *she* was different.

For a moment back there, she hadn't liked Sophie one bit. She felt angry again. Then she shrugged it away. The heck with it. I'll think about my detective game instead. Everything was right up front with that. You didn't have to guess. The numbers, the words, the commands — they were all clear and logical and...pure. Pure, that's what they were. A lot purer than people. People were always hiding from each other behind words they didn't mean. And they make me hide, too, she thought. All of them. My mom and my dad and my teachers — and now Sophie, too. The heck with it. Who needs people anyway? Not me.

She ran down the hall to Mr. Guthrie's room just as the final bell rang.

Minerva glanced at her watch as she sucked the last of the milk through her straw. It made a noise like an empty stomach. Twelve-fifteen. Good. Almost an hour.

Maybe she'd have time to try out some of the neat sound stuff Rick and Angelo had set up. It was really state-of-the-art, with a Winchester drive to handle 10-megabyte hard disks, and some super software. One program, called *Backtalk*, let you store ordinary conversation and play it back later, and at the same time analyzed your voice and showed a picture of it on the monitor, all in spiky clumps. You could get a printout of it, too, and everything — the micro, the drive, and the printer — was plugged into a power bar at the back so you only had to press one switch. Angelo had brought a tape deck from home, Rick had conned the music department out of a speaker and a ball mike, and the two of them had rigged a miniature sound lab on one end of the long desk against the wall.

She pitched the empty carton into a nearby waste-basket and wheeled into the computer room at a dead run — and stopped abruptly before she ran right into Mr. Purcell. One of his first rules, right after school started, was "Students shall not run in the halls."

"Hello, sir," she said.

He frowned at her through his rimless glasses, then turned back to Rick and Mrs. Sinclair. Rick was eating a Mars Bar. Probably his lunch, thought Minerva. Looked like they were into a heavy-duty conference. She walked over to her machine and flipped the switch. The screen glowed mistily, like a summoned ghost, and said READY. Minerva pulled some papers from the pocket of her jeans and started to type.

```
10 REM THE MINERVA PROGRAM
```

Hey man, that looks good, she thought.

```
20 ?"YOU ARE NOW THE FAMOUS DETECTIVE,
   MINERVA SHERLOCK"
```

```
30 ?"YOU RECEIVE A TELEPHONE CALL FROM...
```

"Oh, Minerva, could you spare us a minute?"

Minerva jumped and looked around. Rick was beckoning to her. She rose and went towards him.

"How's the game?" he asked.

"Still has a few bugs."

"Need some help?"

Minerva hesitated. "Uh, no thanks, I don't think so." She hoped she didn't sound rude. "I'd like to work them out on my own, if that's okay."

Rick grinned and turned to the others. "See what I mean? She's a natural. She won't have any problems with the files."

Minerva looked from one to the other, mystified. Purcell was still frowning, but Mrs. Sinclair was her usual friendly self.

"Minerva," she said, "Mr. Purcell wants to streamline our record-keeping and, since we now have both the right machine for the job and the right person for the machine, we'd like to ask you to take it on." She smiled.

"Me?" Minerva looked at her, mouth open in shock.

"You."

"You think I can do it, Mrs. Sinclair?"

"I'm sure you can, Minerva."

"Miss Wright," said Mr. Purcell, arranging his frown. Maybe he sets it every morning when he shaves, thought Minerva. Sticks one wrinkle to the next with Krazy Glue. "Miss Wright," he said again. "As you know, the Board has gone to considerable expense to supply Pinevale students with this impressive array of equipment." He looked around the room with obvious pride. "In all modesty, may I say that it was I who persuaded the Board to approve the funds for this purchase, by guaranteeing that the computers would be used not only as educational instruments, but also as a means to rationalize our files and records to make them compatible with those of other administrations."

Minerva stared at him.

"Do I make myself clear, Miss Wright?"

You gotta be kidding, thought Minerva. But aloud she said, "Yes, sir. All the school stuff that's on paper you want put on the computer."

He looked at her as if his face didn't know what to do with itself. "That is correct, Miss Wright. The office staff can handle much of this, but it is my conviction that volunteer student help, if trustworthy and competent, might profitably be utilized."

Volunteer? That usually meant no pay. Purcell was in his standard miser operating mode. "Yes, sir," she said.

"Mrs. Sinclair and school secretary Mrs. Clark can instruct you in your duties." He nodded at her and left the room.

Minerva glanced at Mrs. Sinclair and Rick. They were both trying not to laugh. "Man oh man, he is somethin' else!" she said.

Then all of them laughed.

But Minerva was pleased. She had a job. A computer job. No money but who cared about that? She'd actually be doing real work on the computer! And why? Because she was the best!

And it wouldn't be work. It would be play.

6

MINERVA did up her jacket and put her hands in her pockets. Cold today. She ducked into the shelter of Pinevale's side door and tried to see James among the kids playing in the Sir Ernest schoolyard.

Where was he? It was after four, and he hadn't shown up. And I still have to get the groceries, she thought, and then make supper, with both Mom and Dad working tonight. So — naturally — he decides to disappear.

She could hear the faint sounds of the band tuning up in the auditorium. Rehearsal again today. She wondered how Sophie was. It had been weeks now, and they hadn't made it up properly. She'd seen Sophie in the halls, and in gym, and sometimes at their lockers, and they'd said "Hi" very politely and carefully. Which made Minerva feel awkward and angry.

But she hadn't felt lonely, except when something funny happened, or something weird, or something awful, or something wonderful. At those times she would forget and think, "Wait'll I tell Soph!" Then she would remember again that she couldn't tell Soph and feel sad. But it always went away after a while.

Anyway, she was so busy with computer stuff she didn't have time for much else. The job was easy — just updating names and addresses and telephone numbers — and she'd learned it in minutes. And her game was getting more and more complicated and more and more fun to put together. No, she hardly even missed Sophie. Maybe this was what happened to friends anyway. Once you had other things to take their place, you didn't really need them any more. And not having friends gives you more time, too, she thought — you don't have to be thinking of what someone else wants. You can just do your own thing. Like computers, for example.

She crossed the yard to Sir Ernest. Maybe James had told somebody to give her a message. A bunch of kids were gathered round the flagpole and she turned towards them.

"Hey, any of you guys seen James Wright?"

They shoved one another and giggled. Then they all backed away from her. What the heck's wrong with them? she wondered. Is my zipper undone or something? One boy took a step toward her and yelled, "He's hangin' around here somewhere!" They all broke up laughing again and watched her expectantly.

A wild shout came out of the sky. "Look out belo-o-ow!" And down the flagpole slid James, landing in a pile of papery leaves at the bottom. He looked up at his sister, delighted with himself. "Hi, Minnie! Just thought I'd drop in!"

"James, you could've killed yourself! One of these days..." She grabbed him but he wriggled free and took off for the shopping centre. "... and don't call me Minnie!" she yelled, racing after him.

She caught up to him, out of breath, just outside her mother's store. It was jammed. All twelve cashiers were busy and the line-ups straggled into the aisles. She looked down the row of cash desks. Her mother was on eleven, the express for sixteen items or less. Her line-up was pretty long, too. Of course, a lot of the regulars went to her because she was so fast and friendly.

But she didn't seem to be either today, Minerva thought as she stood and watched for a minute. Her mother wasn't smiling, and the rhythm of her movements, usually a pleasure to watch, seemed jerky and out of sync, as if she were just learning. Then Minerva knew why. The new machines had been put in. The "smart" registers.

James ducked under the turnstile to kneel by the magazine rack, and Minerva saw him settle down with a couple of comic books. Good, she thought. He'll be easy to find for once. She got closer to desk number eleven, caught her mother's eye and waved. Her mother nodded, signalled her to wait. Her face was marked with strain, lips pressed tight together and a small frown between her eyes. She'd grumbled off and on all week about the new system, which was sort of a surprise because she hardly ever complained, but Minerva hadn't paid much attention. Now she watched, fascinated, and couldn't understand what her mother was upset about.

It was neat! The cashiers hardly had to do a thing! Except for fresh stuff like vegetables and meat, which had to be registered the old way, they just swept everything past the glass scanner. Then the scanner read the Universal Product Code — all those black lines and numbers in a little square on the label — and the whole thing was automatically fed to the computer in the office. In less than a second, too. The computer knew what each code meant and printed it out on your register slip. It was better than your own shopping list. Minerva retrieved a discarded slip from the floor and looked at it. The old ones only had things like GROC and PROD and MT on them. This one had everything. At the top it said "HAVE A SUPER DAY FROM MAPLE LEAF SUPERMARKET." Under that was the store number, 78, and the date. Then the big long list of purchases, like DOLE PINEAPL .59; UNC BEN RICE 1.75; APPLES .825KG (1KG/2.18) 1.80; CHRISTIE BIS 2.09. And at the bottom the register number and the time, 15:46. It was neat!

The line was moving faster now, each item anounced with a beep as it went by the scannér, prices and totals and change flashing in square red digits above the money drawer. Minerva was spellbound, and as she stood there she had a sudden strange vision of what the future might bring: an endless river of groceries flowing across the scanner, all channelled and propelled by a moving belt, billions of bits of information pouring into the computer and out again in instant itemized lists, automatic bagging — and no need for cashiers at all.

In fact, why not go all the way and get rid of the customers? she thought. And even the store. Suppose you had a computer in your living room or kitchen: you could just dial your grocery list to a big food warehouse, and the warehouse computer would send commands to robots A and B — or maybe they'd call them Al and Brenda — and the robots would go and get your order together, and then it would be delivered right to your door by a computerized truck or helicopter.

And then, she thought excitedly as she pushed her fancy further, the warehouse computer could call up the bank computer and tell it to subtract sixty-seven dollars and thirteen cents from your account. And that would be that. No money. No stores. No people. Just machines.

It would sure be faster. And quieter. She listened for a moment to the hundred separate sounds in the store: a crying baby, bacon sizzling at the snack bar, two boys laughing, someone calling "Buggies from outside please", the liquid slap of a mop. All of these sounds, these human sounds, would be gone, and only whirs and beeps and clickings — unheard by anyone, ever — would disturb the silence.

Minerva shivered suddenly and wrenched her mind back to the present. Her mother had put up the "PLEASE USE NEXT REGISTER" sign. Her last customer was an old woman clutching five loaves of bread. She was short and fat, with grey hair pulled into a bun. The three buttonholes of her black overcoat had frayed and then been mended with thread that didn't quite match. Loosely moored in one ear was a hearing aid. She arranged the loaves in a row on the desk and from her pocket fished a handful of coupons clipped from newspapers. These she thrust at Minerva's mother.

"I pay with this," she said.

Victoria Wright pressed the button to start the belt and the bread rolled towards her. The woman held the coupons closer. On each was printed "One loaf Maple Leaf bread, 40 cents with this coupon."

"I pay with this," she repeated.

Minerva's mother smiled, nodded, took the coupons, glanced at them. She frowned a little, then leaned towards the old woman. "These have expired, madam," she said in a low tone.

"I pay with them," said the old woman.

"I'm sorry, madam." Victoria raised her voice slightly. "The coupons expired last Saturday."

"You take. How much else?" asked the old woman, uncomprehending. She opened an old-fashioned black handbag with small straps, the leather shiny and soft from years of use, and plucked from it a tiny change purse. From the purse she took a much-folded two-dollar bill. The only thing left in it, Minerva saw, was a street-car ticket. She glanced at her mother. She had seen it, too.

Swiftly, then, Victoria Wright picked up the loaves of bread, avoiding the scanner, and packed them into two plastic bags. "That will be two dollars, please, madam," she said.

The old woman smoothed the two-dollar bill with hands that were equally wrinkled and offered it, smiling.

"Thank you, madam." Minerva's mother rang up two dollars and handed the old woman her register slip.

"Thank *you*, lady. I see you next week." The woman tucked the bread into a worn cloth shopping bag and walked from the store, her step firm.

Minerva watched as her mother crumpled the coupons and dropped them in the wastebasket, then reached under the cash drawer for her purse. She rang up two dollars and forty-five cents, put that amount into the drawer, turned to her daughter and said, "You didn't see an old lady just buy five loaves of bread for two dollars, did you, Minerva?"

Minerva felt like hugging her mother, but instead

she grinned and said, "Who? Me? Didn't see a thing, Mom!"

Victoria Wright swung a bag from underneath the counter. "Here. Hamburger meat. Buns. Sale on the buns, two packages for ninety-nine. And some bananas, on for fifty-six a kilo today. And the doughnuts were marked down to eighty-nine a dozen. Yesterday's but they're still fresh."

"How do you remember all that, Mom?"

Her mother's mouth twisted. "Hah! Hardly have to remember anything around here any more. All you need for this job now is two arms and enough strength to stand on your feet all day."

"But isn't it easier now, Mom? And there's less chance of making mistakes."

"It's not easier at all! My hands hardly know where to put themselves. And I didn't make mistakes!" Victoria Wright was silent a moment and when she spoke again her voice was fierce. "You know what we are now? Part of a machine, that's what! Part of a machine! And not the important part either!"

Minerva said nothing. She didn't want to argue, but she was sure her mother had it all wrong. Didn't she see, didn't she understand what was happening? Minerva remembered again what Mrs. Sinclair had told them, that the whole world was changing fast, and that people's lives would change, too. All because of the computer. It was a revolution, she'd said, a revolution that could bring more freedom to everybody, and Minerva recalled how her mind had leaped at the words, how she'd caught her breath at such an idea.

She could see it happening right now in her own school. Already Mrs. Clark didn't have to do all kinds of boring stuff by hand, the class schedules were worked out in an hour instead of a week, the student grades and records for every school in the district were safely stored away in the big data bank at the Board office, the resource centre didn't need a card catalogue any more. And Purcell didn't frown as much — the school was saving time, space, and money. All because of the computer.

Mr. Guthrie had used up a whole social studies class talking about it. Half the kids hadn't paid any attention, but Minerva still remembered every word. He'd said it was like another time two hundred years ago when machines started to do jobs that people had done by hand. The Industrial Revolution, he'd called it, and he'd told them there'd been no way to stop it, just as now there was no way to stop the Computer Revolution. People's lives had been changed, had even been turned upside down, but then, as now, there'd been no going back.

Minerva felt part of the newness, the excitement, part of the future, and she saw her mother as part of the past, a bit like those people two centuries ago who had tried to smash all the machines and destroy the inventions. The Luddites, they were called, and they'd marched into factories with sledge-hammers and picks in the darkness of night, leaving wreckage and ruin behind them. Until the government shot some, hanged others, and sent hundreds to prison.

Minerva shook her head. Stupid. The thought of wrecking a computer made her stomach go all tight. It was like murder. She'd just as soon take a hammer to James. She grinned. Not that it hadn't crossed her mind a few times. Besides, it wouldn't matter how many machines you wrecked, you'd never be able to wreck the idea of the machine. Stupid.

She felt as if there were a huge gulf between her mother and herself, and she was impatient and a little sad that this should be so. It seemed to her that her mother was deliberately being stubborn and slow, refusing to understand. She took the bag of groceries without a word.

So okay, she thought. So I can't talk to my mother about the most important thing in my life. Wonderful. Was this part of growing up, too? Leaving people behind? Like her mother, like Sophie? For an instant she felt terribly alone, then she remembered there were others who felt as she did: Rick, Angelo, Mrs. Sinclair, Mr. Guthrie sometimes, even Barbara Fairfax, who was really sharp once she sat down in front of a screen. They understood. And they talked to her in language she understood. They were as excited as she and as bewitched by the power and the dreams of power that lay waiting to be discovered. The future seemed a land without limits, and she felt again that surge of joy as she realized she would be one of those

66

who explored that land, who commanded the future. And she would leave Sophie and her mother and all the rest who were stuck in the past, without regret, without a backward look.

7

```
90 ?"YOU HAVE DEDUCED THAT THERE ARE"

100 ?"THREE PEOPLE WITH THE OPPORTUNITY"

110 ? TO COMMIT THE CRIME"
```

Better check it, thought Minerva. She typed in RUN. The game program scrolled up the screen and then stopped abruptly.

```
SYNTAX ERROR LINE 110
```

"Oh, shoot," she whispered. She listed the program again and checked the offending line. Um. Forgot the quotes. Getting tired. She rubbed her eyes and looked at her watch. Four-thirty. Soon be time to meet James. She wondered where he went after school these days. Probably climbing up and down tall buildings. Or hanging out at The Gamekeeper's, unless Hofmann the Hulk was there. Mom and Dad would be mad if they ever found out. But they won't, she assured herself. James'll keep quiet.

She glanced around the room. Not too many here today. Most of the kids had gone to the basketball game at Naismith Junior High. Angelo, earphones on his head and a stopwatch in one hand, kept stopping and starting the tape deck and making notes on some graph paper. Minerva had listened to some of the stuff he'd composed on the computer, and it was really weird, with rhythms and melodies unlike anything she'd ever heard. Barbara had been fooling around with the *Backtalk* program, but she was gone now.

Minerva stood up and stretched. Time to do the update for Mrs. Clark. Everything had to be done before the report cards came out tomorrow. Not that I'm all that wild to get my report, she thought. Pickle's practically said right out loud that I'll fail gym. And family studies and socials are disaster areas. She sighed, grabbed the manila folder she'd picked up from Mrs. Clark's desk, and walked over to one of the terminals connected to the Board's mainframe. She sat down, smiling briefly at Rick beside her. He didn't look up. He was eating corn chips and mumbling away to himself as usual. Probably hadn't even seen her. His fingers pecked at the keys like nervous birds as he squinted at the screen. Minerva was sure the school could burn down around him and he'd never notice. A real hacker. And a nice guy. She liked him.

She switched on. The monitor flashed with green print.

OXBRIDGE DISTRICT DATA STORAGE
AND RETRIEVAL SYSTEM
ODDSTARS Rev·2

NAME?   MINERVA WRIGHT, she responded.
PASSWORD?   FINGERS, she typed.
OK, signalled the machine.

The prompt came up and waited, blinking at her. She gave it a command.

L· STUD·DIR·

The computer searched its memory for half a second and then obeyed.

FILE STUDENT DIRECTORY, it said, and then the screen began to fill with the names, addresses and telephone numbers of all the students in the district. Minerva scrolled through the list till she found those needing changes and began to enter the new information.

Mark and Barbara came in with their arms around each other. Barbara's hair was crazier than ever, Minerva noticed. She'd bleached it blonde, to match Mark's, but it had turned out sort of silver with shiny pink streaks. They walked past her and Rick to the sound lab.

"Hi, Minerva," said Barbara. Minerva lifted a

hand. Barbara reached back and flipped the power bar switch, then sat down between Angelo and Rick. The red light glowed on the Winchester, and she asked for *Backtalk*.

"We just came in to get Mark's voice-print," Barbara continued. "He's got one of mine, and we're going to put them on matching T-shirts." She lined up the paper in the nearby printer, then checked the microphone and held it up to Mark.

"What'll I say?" asked Mark. Then, leering at her, he said in a deep voice, "Hands off. Trespassers will be boiled in oil. Property of Mark Hofmann." The two of them giggled as they watched the jagged acoustical pattern come up on the screen. Barbara pressed a key, and the pattern vanished; she pressed another, and it began to reappear on the paper.

Minerva turned back to her own keyboard and checked the revisions she'd made. She was about to power down when she noticed another page in the manila folder. Another address change. Mrs. Clark must have added it at the last minute. "Ms. Hilde-garde Dill, 21 Windy Lane, Suite 307, same code," read Minerva. Then she read it again. That wasn't a student, that was Pickle!

Minerva sat back. Hildegarde. Wow. Some name... Wonder why Pickle's moving... Mrs. Clark looked after the teacher updates... She must have put this in the wrong folder... Minerva had never even been told about any file other than the student directory. A smile grew on her face and a feeling of excitement gripped her. Wonder if I could find the file, she thought. Wonder if my access code's high enough... Bet I could if I tried... Let's see... If I asked for a catalogue of all the files...

She glanced quickly to her left. Rick was still gazing at his screen. Barbara and Mark were gazing at each other. And Angelo wasn't gazing at anything — he was listening to a tape with his eyes shut. Minerva touched the C key. The screen instantly filled with filenames and she felt once again that exultation, familiar now but as keen as ever, that sense of power and control. She scanned the list. Ah! STAFFDOC. That had to be it. But there were several files with that name, each with a letter attached. Which one? She shrugged and typed "Q. STAFFDOC.A"

Immediately, as fast as thought, a list of teachers' names and addresses appeared. All laid out in front of her. Minerva felt enormously clever. She almost laughed out loud with pleasure. She'd found it all by herself. It was scrolling to the Cs and Ds now, and she hit the HOLD key. Dill... Dill... There it was. She moved the cursor and made the change. Her eyes strayed across the screen and stopped abruptly at the right margin. There were figures opposite each name. With dollar signs in front of them. Minerva gasped. She'd found her way into some kind of salary data base. For the whole District! Oh-oh. I've got a feeling I'm some place I shouldn't be, she thought.

Better get out. Right away. She glanced sideways at Rick, aware of a silence. She was so accustomed to his constant muttering that the room seemed strange without it. He was looking at her.

"Anything wrong, Minerva?" He smiled, vague as ever.

"No," she said quickly. "Everything's okay."

He turned back to his own screen and Minerva relaxed. Now to put back Dill's old address and nobody will ever know, she thought. But what *was* the old address? It had gone right out of her head. Maybe it's in one of the other staff files, she thought. She asked for the catalogue again and it spread before her on the monitor. And then she heard, from directly behind her, the soft grey voice of Mr. Purcell.

"Miss Wright."

Minerva jumped up and whirled around, punching the CLEAR key on the way. Her chair fell back and hit Mr. Purcell's knees. His mouth tightened further, and Minerva thought wildly that he'd swallowed his lips. Her heart hammered in her throat. What had he seen? How long had he been standing there? From the corner of her eye she saw Barbara and Mark edge away from the desk and sneak out of the room. And then she saw James, trying to hide behind Mr. Purcell, his glance darting fearfully from Mark to the principal to her.

"Miss Wright."

"Yes, sir." Minerva picked up the chair.

"This young person claims to be a relative of yours. Is that the case?" He propelled James forward as if he were handling something unpleasant.

"Yes, sir. He's my little brother. James." Oh man, what had the spaz done now?

"Do you know where I discovered your little brother James?"

For about the thousandth time in her life, Minerva wondered why adults always asked questions they already knew the answers to. Weird.

"No, sir."

Mr. Purcell smiled. At least Minerva hoped it was a smile. Maybe he was just baring his teeth. Before he bit her. Who knew? She took a chance and smiled back.

Mr. Purcell spoke. "In a singularly foolhardy deed of what he imagined was derring-do, not to mention a criminal act of which prosecution is the most likely consequence, your little brother James was apprehended while attempting to scale the wall outside this window."

Minerva heard Rick chuckle. She threw him a grateful glance.

"This is not a laughing matter, Richard!" said Mr. Purcell.

"Sorry, Uncle Pete." Rick grinned and popped the top of a Diet Pepsi. Its gentle buzz was the only sound in the room.

"Well, Miss Wright?"

Minerva stared at him helplessly. "Well, uh, you

see, sir, James thinks Spiderman is the greatest, and he practises all the time, you wouldn't believe the stuff he does, he climbs buildings, walls, flagpoles..."

The rest of her sentence was lost in an eerie howling followed by a chorus of shrill and terrified bleats, as if animals were in pain, and then something that sounded like a bad car crash.

Mr. Purcell's cheeks quivered and his chin dropped onto his tie. "Wha—what was that?" he whispered.

"It's just Angelo's project, sir," answered Minerva. "Ange!" She reached over and punched Angelo in the arm. He took off his earphones and stared at her. "Ange! Turn it down!"

Rick was laughing so hard he could hardly talk. "What's the name of that one, Angelo? Concerto for the MX missile?"

Angelo looked hurt. "It's *O Canada*," he said. "Didn't you guys recognize it? I just changed a few things, that's all."

Mr. Purcell was breathing very hard. Minerva watched his tie-clip rise and fall for a while. Finally he spoke, and she had to strain to hear him.

"I would like this room empty of all students," he whispered. "Now."

"But I..." began Angelo.

"Now," said Mr. Purcell.

Oh, terrific, thought Minerva. Now how am I going to fix that file the way it was? I'll have to do it somehow. Before Mrs. Clark finds out. She turned off the terminal and stuffed the pages back in the manila folder.

With Mr. Purcell's glare following her, she grabbed James by the neck and hurried from the room.

"What a grump!" said Angelo outside.

"He just doesn't appreciate fine music, Ange." She smiled at him, all the while wondering how she was going to get rid of him. She *had* to get back to that file.

James stopped abruptly. She turned around, ready to yell at him. He was staring down the hall in terror. She looked ahead. At the end of the corridor she saw Mark opening his locker. James broke loose from her and ran back the way they had come. With a quick wave to Angelo, Minerva took off after him.

She caught up to him at the bank of lockers just opposite the computer room. Five or six had no locks. She yanked one open and shoved James inside. "Just keep quiet till I tell you!" she whispered. Then she folded herself into the locker next to his, once again cursing her long legs. Now I know what a pretzel feels like, she thought. She nudged the door until a crack of light showed, and peered out. By twisting her neck till it hurt, she could focus on the computer room across the hall.

She heard voices and saw one trouser leg. Dark grey. Pinstripe. Mr. Purcell. Then she saw the other leg, and finally the rest of him, walking away from her now, down the hall. She nudged the door a little more and saw him go into the boys' washroom. Probably checking to see if somebody swiped the toilet paper, Minerva thought. She waited, counting by threes to make the time go faster, her eyes flicking back and forth from the computer room to the washroom. Rick must still be working; she remembered he had to teach a night school class later and was thankful. Maybe he wouldn't lock up. Maybe she could get in and out fast, make up some story if he got curious. She took a deep breath and was about to step into the hall when she heard footsteps, soft and secret footsteps, as if the owner of the feet didn't want to be seen or heard. Minerva closed the door a bit and put one eye against the crack.

It was Barbara. Creeping down the corridor on tip-toe, looking carefully to her left and right, glancing over her shoulder. What was she after? What was she doing here? Then Rick came out of the computer room and Barbara ducked out of sight behind a trophy case. Rick stood still for a moment, listening for something, then walked to the stairs, his crepe-soled shoes squeaking on the tile floor. Minerva heard him go down, the sound of his progress diminishing until there was silence. Silence. Weird to be in the school when it was so quiet. She wondered where Barbara was. Maybe she'd gone. If so, now's my chance, thought Minerva. She edged the door open slightly.

No. Past her straining vision went part of a nose, then part of a left ear with a giant gold earring attached, and then a bunch of silvery spikes smudged here and there with pink. Barbara. Minerva shifted her body noiselessly. Every muscle she owned complained. She watched Barbara glide into the computer room. What the heck was going on?

There was a faint tapping noise right beside her and she jumped in fright. James. She'd forgotten all about him. She hissed at the metal wall between them. "Shut up, James! Just shut up!" Then she heard footsteps approaching once more. This place was busier than the subway at rush hour.

She pulled the locker door tight and tried to lean back. The shelf above her head pressed down hard on her neck. One hip seemed higher than the other, and she couldn't feel her left foot. Maybe it had died. If she didn't get out of here soon, maybe all of her would. She'd be stuck here forever, and then one day the people who dug up old ruins would find her at last, her body all twisted in knots, skinnier than ever, and they'd wonder who she was, and why she was buried standing up in a metal box... And everybody would be sorry. Pickle, even Purcell maybe. And her Mom and Dad. And Sophie. Sophie would really feel bad...

She felt her eyes blur with tears and snapped out of her daydream, shaking her head at her own craziness.

The footsteps stopped. Right in front of her. She heard breathing. It wasn't hers. Then a voice. She managed to press one ear against the door.

"Miss Fairfax, I thought you'd left long ago." It was Purcell. Minerva could hear the frown.

"Just leaving now, sir, I lost an earring, thought it might be here."

Earring? What was she talking about? Minerva twisted her head till it was almost upside down and peered through one of the little slits on the locker door.

An earring, golden, huge, and outrageous, dangled right in front of her. Barbara was lying. She always wore just one, never two. And everybody knew it. Except Purcell, apparently. Barbara was lying. But why?

"Good night, sir. 'Night, Rick. See ya."

Rick? Minerva's shoulders slumped further back. Rick was back. This was getting ridiculous. Also hot. She could feel sweat forming under her hair at the back, and her upper lip tasted salty. She chewed at her thumbnail, then remembered she'd made a resolution not to do that any more. She wondered what time it was and held her watch close to her face. The numbers, faintly luminous, blinked at her. Five-twenty-six and thirty-seven seconds, thirty-eight, thirty-nine...

"Give you a lift home, Richard?"

"No, thanks, Uncle Pete, I'll pick up some food at the mall and come back for the evening class."

Food? Rick never ate food, not real food. He'd likely get a package of Twinkies and another Diet Pepsi, thought Minerva. But this meant — at last! — that she could get into the computer room and change the file.

Then she almost cried out in rage and disappointment.

"Just wait till I lock up, Uncle Pete, and I'll walk out with you."

The sound of a key turning. A click and a jingling noise. She felt her breath go out of her like air from a balloon.

Now she'd have to wait till tomorrow and hope that

neither Mrs. Clark nor anyone else would discover she'd messed around with a staff file. She sighed. It was called "B & E," she remembered. Break and enter. That's what she'd done. She was a burglar. A criminal.

She opened the locker door and looked up and down the corridor. All clear. She stepped out, her body stiff and aching, and tapped her fingers on the adjacent locker.

"Come on, James."

No answer. No sound. No movement. Alarmed, Minerva swung the door open.

James was asleep, his knees making a pillow for his head, his face turned towards her and innocent of mischief. Minerva looked at him and felt old. She bent down and shook him gently. He stirred and smiled up at her.

"You're safe now, James," she said. "Let's go home."

8

"CARR, Paula," Mr. Guthrie said.

Minerva watched Paula get up, smooth her skirt even though it didn't have any wrinkles in it, and walk to the front to get her report card.

"Excellent, Paula," said Mr. Guthrie. "As usual."

Paula smirked.

Bet she got a hundred in everything, thought Minerva. What a creep! She had the best notes in the class, and she never loaned them to anybody.

"DeLuz, Angelo."

Angelo went forward.

"Yes, here you are, Angelo, still some work to do in phys. ed., eh my boy? But it'll come, I'm sure, yes..."

This was one of those times, mused Minerva, that she wished her name didn't start with W. Mr. Guthrie always took the scenic route through the alphabet, making little exclamations along the way. And every now and then he'd stop altogether, his voice fading away like a bad radio station. Minerva was sure he just started thinking about something else and forgot where he was.

"Moncada, Miguel. Fine work in social studies, Miguel, I'm glad to see...now where is your report card, I had it here..."

Miguel stared at him in bewilderment. "You just gave it to me, sir, see?" He held it in front of Mr. Guthrie's face. "It's here, sir!"

"Oh, yes, good, now who is next? Ah, here we are, Palermo, Luisa. Very good indeed, Luisa, you make me proud..."

A forest of hands waved at him. "Sir!" "Sir!" "Sir!"

He glanced up. "Yes?"

Minerva and six others yelled, "Luisa's not here today, sir!"

"Not here? Well, well, now that's strange, she was here yesterday, at least I believe so, I'm sure I remember her...well..." And he smiled sweetly at the class.

"Rogers, William..."

Minerva let her mind roam. She'd been too late this morning to speak to Mrs. Clark. Hope nobody gets too mad, she thought. I didn't mean to do it, after all. They should have better systems, a better way of protecting those files. If I could get into them, other people could... Wonder why Barbara snuck into the computer room... Wonder if Purcell frowns in his sleep, too... Wonder what I got in gym?

"Tomasino, Tom," said Mr. Guthrie. There was a smothered snicker. Minerva grinned. All the kids called him Tom-Tom. As he walked back to his desk some of the boys drummed on their desks. He bowed.

Maybe I can finish up my game program today, Minerva thought. Wish we could get a credit for computers this term. Or substitute it for something I'm not so good in. Which is just about everything. She grew gloomy again.

"Wasylenko, Yvonne, yes, wonderful English mark, Yvonne, the highest I've ever seen..."

Minerva tensed, and her stomach throbbed with worry. Stupid, she thought. I can't do anything about it now.

"Yakota, Jane..."

Minerva sat up straighter, frowning slightly. She looked at Mr. Guthrie. He was gazing out the window. He'd finished with the report cards. But where was hers? She waited a moment, then raised her hand.

"Sir, I didn't get mine!"

A girl yelled out, "Take mine then!" and a boy whispered, "See me later, baby!" There was scattered laughter. Mr. Guthrie stared at Minerva. He looked perplexed. He turned to his desk and riffled through the papers lying in unruly heaps, all the while muttering, "How odd! How very odd!"

He was still riffling, still muttering, when the bell rang. Gym was next, Minerva remembered with a familiar dread. She dashed to her locker and grabbed her gymsuit. Sophie was nearby, dialling her combination. Minerva looked sideways at her, and their eyes met. Sophie hastily looked away before Minerva had a chance to open her mouth. She longed to say "Hi, Soph!" in the old and easy way; she would have liked to tell her about Purcell catching James climbing up the wall, and getting trapped in the locker, and Barbara lying, and about not getting a report today. Sophie would laugh and listen and worry with her. At least the old Sophie would have. Minerva watched as Sophie turned to speak to Pat Leach. Bubblehead First Class Leach. Can't understand that, Minerva brooded. Why anyone would want to talk to her, assuming she's capable of speech, for longer than thirty seconds, is a mystery. She shrugged. The heck with it! Who cares? She ran into the gym.

Miss Dill was in the centre of the room punishing an innocent basketball. Slap, slap, slap it went, as she bounced it on the varnished floor, each time returning as if on a string to the hand that propelled it. And Pickle wasn't even looking at it. For an instant Minerva was filled with admiration. It was like watching a perfect machine.

Then dread took over again. Basketball was always a disaster. She was good at free shots, but that was all. Unless she was all by herself. If she stood still and concentrated on the net, with no one breathing all over her or flapping their silly arms in her face, she scored every time, from almost anywhere on the court. But otherwise she was hopeless. And everybody knew it. She chewed at her thumbnail as the teams were chosen. She checked her shoelaces. Both tied. Didn't mean a thing. Sometimes she was convinced they had a vicious little life of their own, because even with double knots they could magically loosen, lie in wait, then trip her when she wasn't looking. And everybody else was. Which was when everybody else laughed. And she didn't...

Pickle blew her whistle, and Minerva moved out onto the floor. She was left guard, assigned to Patricia Airhead. Terrific. Today was shaping up into a real horror movie. Airhead grinned and leapt to the right. Minerva stumbled after her. Everybody was yelling their heads off. The ball flew so fast from one blue suit to another that Minerva never knew where it was. She kept her eyes fixed on Airhead, trying to be her shadow, and waving her arms like a tree in a hurricane. She'd never managed to stop a pass yet, but she figured she'd better do what the rest of them were doing. It was camouflage, she knew: act like the people around you and maybe nobody — especially Pickle, she hoped — would notice you.

Except that Pickle seemed to be watching her every move. Minerva could feel those eyes on her, boring into her back like a laser. Any moment now her ribs would crumble to ashes and her blood vanish in a red mist. She was abruptly aware of her arms, her legs, her muscles and bones and their wrapper of skin; the endless methodical pump of her heart; the busy nerves making notes on temperature and the unseen rub of air and the soft tingle of cloth as her fingers brushed

Patricia's shoulder — and struck by wonder at her body's miraculous hardware, she stopped moving altogether. Then Airhead ran right into her, and she thought as she fell that her hardware might be okay, but her software was really lousy. The original Minerva program just didn't work very well.

She landed hard. Miss Dill's whistle shrilled painfully. The girls stood as if turned to stone. The gym was silent, and when the PA system stuttered it seemed louder than usual.

"Miss Dill, please come to the office. Minerva Wright, come to the office." Mr. Purcell's voice was grim and ceremonial, each word marching into the room as if to the slow beat of a drum. Minerva half expected to hear him add, "And there you will be hanged by the neck until you are dead. May God have mercy on your soul!" She got scared all over again.

Miss Dill stood over her, swinging the whistle in a languid arc. In her hands it seemed a deadly weapon. Minerva scrambled to her feet. Why is she looking at me like that? she wondered. Pickle's eyes were more alive than Minerva had ever seen them, and her mouth curved upwards in a strange smile.

"Michaloff!"

Sophie detached herself from the group and came to where Minerva stood. Miss Dill handed her the whistle and said, "You referee the game until I get back, Michaloff. This shouldn't take long." And her lips did that funny thing again, which Minerva couldn't really call a smile. It was more like the expression she'd seen on skulls at the big Museum downtown. She felt a tremor go through her, and then the quick touch of Sophie's hand on her arm.

"Come along, Wright!"

Minerva went along. In misery and in mushrooming panic. She didn't know what had happened — and Pickle wasn't about to tell her — but it didn't look good. No words were exchanged as she followed the green jogging suit up the stairs, down the hall, which had always seemed so long before today, into the office, past the curious eyes of Mrs. Clark, to stand at last in front of Mr. Purcell.

She glanced furtively around the room. Mr. Guthrie stood by the window, staring at the floor, hands behind his back. He seemed upset. Rick leaned against one wall, and he grinned at her as their eyes met. Mr. Purcell sat behind his desk, his frown securely in place, one hand holding a printout.

"Miss Wright."

"Yes, sir."

"Do you find it odd that you did not receive your report card this morning?"

Minerva looked at the people in the room as if she might find an answer in their faces. "Yes, sir," she said. What was going on? Her mouth was dry. Her armpits were wet. She was suddenly aware of her rumpled gymsuit and the long, brown, bare legs sticking out of it. She felt embarrassed and shy all at once and shifted nervously from one foot to the other.

"Did you for one moment believe, Miss Wright, that

what you did would go undetected?" His voice throbbed with contempt.

"I—I didn't mean to get into that file, sir, I..." Minerva began.

Purcell interrupted her. "You didn't mean to," he mimicked. "And, Miss Wright, I suppose you didn't mean to alter your mark in physical education." He shook the printout at her, and Minerva saw it was her report card.

She stared at him, astonished. "But sir, I..."

Again he interrupted. "Miss Dill, what is Miss Wright's grade this term?"

Minerva turned to look at Pickle. Her eyes were all glittery again, like sequins on leather. She cleared her throat importantly. "I gave her fifty, Mr. Purcell. Rather more than she deserved, I might add." She gave a little laugh. "I do try to be generous with the girls."

Minerva's mouth fell open. Generous? Generous? Scrooge was Santa Claus compared to Pickle! Swiftly she turned back to the principal. "But sir, I didn't change my mark, I wouldn't think of doing that, I..."

He held out the report card to her. "What is your physical education mark, Miss Wright?"

Minerva scanned the printout, her eyes widening in disbelief. She swallowed. Her mouth still felt like a blotter. Finally she whispered, "Seventy, sir."

Pickle snorted. Minerva saw Mr. Guthrie look at Miss Dill as if she'd let him down somehow. Then he shook his head and said "Hildegarde" in a low voice, but Pickle didn't answer him.

"Can you explain the discrepancy, Miss Wright?" asked Purcell.

Minerva wasn't sure what "discrepancy" meant, but right now she couldn't explain anything to anybody. She wasn't sure she was awake; all of this was like a nightmare. She made her face go blank and tried to find the secret place in her mind where no one could touch her, but she seemed to have forgotten the way. Her legs felt weak as water. She forced them straight, stared at Purcell, and said, "No, sir."

"Mr. Guthrie, do you have something to say?"

Mr. Guthrie blew his nose and smiled at her. Minerva looked back at him, a plea written plain on her face. "Mr. Purcell, it's been my experience, as far as I can recollect, which is, as you know, a number of years now, and certainly I've come to know this student rather well, even in the two or is it three months now she's been in my class... Yes, my goodness, it's nearly three months, isn't it..." He stopped and then with a great effort he seemed to recollect what he wished to say. "Minerva's an honest young woman, Mr. Purcell. I can't believe she did this!"

Far inside herself Minerva smiled. He's on my side, she thought, and felt a dangerous softness creep over her. She pushed it away. She couldn't let them see it.

"Thank you, Mr. Guthrie. However, I fear your faith in Miss Wright is based more on fuzzy sentiment than on hard evidence." He made a little tent with his fingers, and went on. "You all know I am a fair-minded man. I have no desire to condemn where there has been no crime. Accordingly, I asked Mr. Campbell to investigate." He nodded at Rick. "Would you be kind enough to show us, Mr. Campbell, what you found this morning?"

Rick pulled himself away from the wall and spread a long printout on Mr. Purcell's desk. He grinned at Minerva, then shrugged as if to say he was sorry.

"And now would you explain this, Mr. Campbell, making a brave attempt to use understandable English?" asked Mr. Purcell.

"Sure, Uncle Pete." He leaned over the printout. "Minerva logged on to ODDSTARS mainframe at 16:33:41, keyed in her ID, and called up the doc file..." He stopped as Mr. Purcell held up his hand.

"English, Rick, English. Remember? You learned it as a child."

Rick squinted at him in surprise, then with thinly veiled scorn. He threw a glance at Minerva and shrugged again. "She got access to the Oxbridge District Data Storage and Retrieval System at about four-thirty, and identified herself with her name and password." He pointed at the printout. "Next she asked the computer to list the contents of the Student Directory file so she could update it." He pointed. "Then, at 16:41:03, I mean, uh, about twenty minutes to five, she asked to see the complete catalogue of all the files."

"Why would she do that?" asked Mr. Guthrie.

Minerva opened her mouth to say something, but Mr. Purcell spoke first. "It's obvious, isn't it, Guthrie? She wanted to get into another file, one where she had no business being." He gave Minerva a disdainful stare. Miss Dill did, too.

Minerva looked from one to the other. They were all talking about her as if she weren't there, as if she were invisible. She remembered how she had always wanted to be part of the crowd, to fit in so well nobody would notice her. Now it had happened. And she didn't know whether to laugh or cry.

"Continue, Rick," said Mr. Purcell.

"Do I have to, Uncle Pete?" Rick looked at Minerva. "She's one of my buddies," he said softly, and Minerva's eyes blurred a little.

"Continue," repeated Mr. Purcell. "I am a fair-minded man, and I wish all the evidence to be known."

Rick hesitated. He rubbed the back of his neck. Minerva saw a new pimple starting to bloom and then wondered why she'd noticed it. Rick went on in a voice so low they bent forward to hear. "Well, it looks like she got into a staff file about ten to five..."

There was a short chorus of gasps. Mr. Guthrie fidgeted, his face troubled. And Pickle moved in, her eyes full of black light, and her mouth slightly open as she bent over the printout. Minerva watched, feeling remote and unreal once more. It was hopeless. They'd never believe anything she said. They'd already judged her and come to a verdict.

Rick unrolled the last part of the printout. "And then, at 17:07:52 — I mean about eight minutes after five — she logged on to the student grades, I guess... I'm not sure just how she did it...but there's her ID and the time, see?" He pointed again.

Minerva stared at Rick. He looked back at her and lifted one shoulder helplessly. What was he talking about? Student grades were level four access, and she only had level six. I know I'm smart but I'm not that smart, she thought. Besides, I wasn't even in the room then! What was happening here? Minerva began to be terribly afraid.

"Mr. Purcell, sir, that's not true!" Her voice was louder than she wanted it to be, but she plunged on. "Don't you remember, sir? You came in the computer room at about five? With James? And you sent me home! Don't you remember, sir?"

"And did you go home, Miss Wright?" he asked, with a slight twitching of his mouth.

Minerva gazed at him. She didn't know what to say. They were all looking at her: Purcell, Dill, Mr. Guthrie, Rick. She felt trapped. The room was silent, waiting.

"Did you go home at five o'clock, Miss Wright?" asked Purcell again, in a whisper that seemed a shout. Miss Dill leaned forward and balanced on the balls of her feet as if she might pounce.

"Not...not right exactly at five, sir," said Minerva, and her shoulders sagged. It was no use. They wouldn't believe her, even if she told the absolute truth. Which was pretty far out anyway. Hiding in a locker? Waiting to sneak into the computer room? She didn't even believe herself any more.

"I don't think we need to hear the rest," said Mr. Purcell. Minerva glanced at him. His cheeks had little spots of red on top of the grey. And Pickle looked as if she'd just polished off her favourite meal. Uncooked human flesh. Mr. Guthrie was very busy examining the toes of his shoes. And Rick had taken off his thick glasses to wipe them on his shirt and couldn't see her even if he'd wanted to.

"I have given some thought to appropriate punishment for this most serious offense," said Mr. Purcell. "I considered suspension..." Mr. Guthrie murmured in distress, and Purcell frowned at him. "... but such a measure struck me as counter-productive." He paused. "Besides, as you well know, I am a fair-minded man. Therefore, I have decided upon the following: one, Miss Wright is to be removed from the computer class; two, Miss Wright is prohibited access to all computers and the computer room until further notice, a prohibition you will see to, Mr. Campbell; three, a natural consequence of one and two, Miss Wright will no longer update any school records, since it is a position of trust and she has violated that trust; and four, a suggestion I owe to Miss Dill" — they bowed and smiled at each other like old-fashioned dancers — "Miss Wright will serve a month of detentions under Miss Dill's supervision, which may indeed bring about that increase in her physical education mark she evidently so desperately desires." He made a noise that in normal human beings might be laughter.

Minerva felt sick. She couldn't seem to think straight, and her hands and feet were terribly cold. All she wanted to do was to get out, get away, far away from these people, and be by herself. In a ragged whisper she said, "May I be excused?"

"One moment, Miss Wright. You'll want your report card." He held it out to Pickle. "Perhaps you'd care to make the necessary correction, Miss Dill?"

Minerva watched as Pickle crossed out the damning and mysterious 70 and with a faint flourish of her pen inked in the number 50. She handed it to Minerva and said, "We'll begin to improve this today after school, Wright."

Minerva took it and looked around the room at each of them. Then she said, very carefully so her voice wouldn't break, "I didn't do it. I didn't do it!"

She turned and ran from the office.

9

GYM should be over by now, Minerva thought. Just as well. She didn't feel like answering any stupid questions, especially from Patricia and the rest of the jocks. She slipped into the deserted change room and sat down on the bench. All at once she began to shake, and her whole body hurt, like the time she'd had the flu. She leaned back against the wall and closed her eyes, overcome by a terrible tiredness. What a mess! What a mess! And nobody to talk to about it, nobody to help her. She felt as if something she had owned and loved was broken, and suddenly she longed to take all the pieces to her father and say, "Daddy fix." But he couldn't fix this, she knew. She could feel tears beginning, but she clenched her teeth and willed them away. No way she'd cry here! No way she'd cry at all! Her hands curled into fists, and she started to hit the bench in a slow, steady rhythm. She almost didn't hear the faint and uncertain whisper.

"Minerva?"

She jumped in alarm and stared up into the dark eyes of Sophie, now wide with concern.

"What happened, Min?"

"Soph, what are you doing here? You should be in class!"

"I skipped." Sophie smiled a little. She seemed proud of herself.

"Sophie Michaloff skipped a class? You've never skipped in your life!"

"Always a first time." Sophie looked around nervously. "But we better split. If Pickle comes in..." She drew a finger across her throat.

Minerva grabbed her clothes, and the two of them dashed across the hall to the washroom. Minerva tripped only once, just as they got safely inside. They started to giggle, looked at each other, and stopped. Neither said anything for a moment, then Minerva blurted, "Oh, Soph, I'm in trouble, deep trouble!" Her voice caught, and something within her, some hard and lonely thing, cracked and gave way. She reached out blindly and felt Sophie's hand grab hers.

"Min, what happened? Tell me! I'm your friend!"

Minerva gulped back a sob. "How can you be my friend when I'm such a jerk?"

Sophie grinned. "I have this weakness for jerks, I guess. Can't resist a first-class jerk. Give me a jerk and I'm happy. Especially tall, skinny jerks. Who trip a lot. Named Minerva."

Minerva started to laugh, and it got all mixed up with crying, then Sophie started to cry, and it got all mixed up with laughing. And neither of them could stop until at last they were holding their sides, out of breath, and Sophie said, "First good laugh I've had since..."

"Since I became a teenage jerk?" asked Minerva.

"You got it, kid! And now, will you kindly tell me what kind of trouble you're in?"

Minerva did. Sophie interrupted a few times to ask a question, and to whoop with glee over Minerva and James hiding in the lockers. When Minerva finished, she was quiet for several minutes. Then she said, "So they believe the computer instead of you?"

Minerva looked startled. "Well, yeah. I guess. But why shouldn't they? My ID's all over the files, the time checked out, and who else but me would care about my phys. ed. mark? They're just being logical, Soph."

"Yep. They're perfectly logical — and perfectly wrong. Just like the computer."

"Aw, c'mon, Soph! A computer just does what somebody tells it to do..." She stopped in mid-sentence and frowned.

"So it changed your mark because somebody told it to," said Sophie. "And the somebody wasn't you, so who was it?"

"I don't know." Minerva pulled on her jeans and

T-shirt. "But I'm going to find out. She looked at Sophie. "I...I know I've got a heck of a nerve, Soph, but...will you help me? You're the only one who believes me. And the only one I can trust."

Sophie's face split in a wide grin. "Minerva, you couldn't keep me away!"

"Be sure to check the pockets, Minerva." Victoria Wright's soft voice echoed in the basement laundry room as she and Minerva sorted the dirty clothes from two orange garbage bags. "Last week I found a ball-point pen and a package of gum — after they'd gone through wash, rinse and spin-dry." She chuckled.

Minerva was trying to get hold of the toes in James's socks. She could never figure out how he got every single sock all bunched up into a little ball, with the toe stuffed into the heel part, and the heel part stuffed into the leg part. When you dumped them out on the floor they rolled, they actually rolled! Sometimes she was sure he did it on purpose, as part of his long-range plan to drive her completely out of her mind.

She came to her own jeans and felt in the pockets. Her hand closed on a folded piece of paper, and she pulled it out and opened it. Her game program. She sighed. She'd probably never finish it now.

They loaded the clothes into three washers, fed them soap and quarters, and sat down to wait on a nearby bench. Ever since some crook had swiped her mother's lace tablecloth last summer, right out of the dryer, they'd never left their laundry unguarded.

"What's that, Min?"

Minerva still had the program in her hand. "This? Oh, just a little game I was trying to work out on the computer." She folded it up, hoping her mother wouldn't get too nosy. She couldn't tell her parents. Not yet. She'd tell them later maybe. After it was all over, after she found out who had messed up her life. Who was just as much a crook as the person who stole their tablecloth.

"They don't scare you at all, Minerva?"

"Huh? What, Mom? Sorry, I was thinking about something else."

"Computers. All the fancy new gadgets. Seems to me they're taking over the world."

Minerva looked at her mother. Did she know? Why was she talking about computers? She answered carefully. "No, I'm not scared of them, Mom. Might as well be scared of a pencil or a TV, or...or that washing machine. It's got a little program in it that somebody wrote out, just like this one." She held up the piece of paper. "I think they're great. And the only thing they're taking over is a lot of the work. Pretty soon everybody's life will be easier and happier."

"That so, Min?" Her mother smiled lopsidedly. "Can't come soon enough for me. I have to grit my teeth to get through the day now."

"The new registers?"

Her mother nodded. "The whole store has changed. We used to laugh a lot, make jokes, talk to the customers. It was like... like family." She stared into space, her face gloomy. "Not any more." She got up and with swift economical movements put the wash in the big dryer, slipped two quarters in the slot, and slammed the door.

"Not any more." She sat down again. "Maybe the work does get done faster, like they say." She paused and rubbed her hands along the smooth skin of her arms as she searched for words. "But something's gone from it now. Something in the work that made it *my* work, that's gone." She looked at her daughter, her eyes bright with feeling. "And I was good, Minerva! I knew every price, I knew all the specials, I was faster than the register most of the time."

Minerva thought suddenly that her mother was talking to her as if they were both the same age, as if they were friends. She kept still, wanting it to continue.

Her mother gazed again into the shadows of the laundry room. "Did I ever tell you the story of my Uncle George?" she asked, and the sound of her voice was almost like singing, with a dark and gentle pulse that was always there when she spoke of home. Her "remembering voice," Minerva called it, and she could almost see the hot blue sky and the white beaches that had no end.

"Uncle George played the guitar in a little restaurant down by the water, and he was a happy man. He knew all the tunes, and he knew all the people who came to hear the tunes. Never had money, but never wanted it. All Uncle George ever wanted was to play the guitar in that little restaurant down by the water. He was a happy man.

"One day the little restaurant was bought by some folks who had a mind to change things. First thing you know they brought in some fancy new disco stuff and a big box of records, and they said to Uncle George, 'George, no more guitar, you got to play these records instead.'

"And he did, for a while. But he didn't like the tunes much, and he didn't know the people who came to dance to the tunes. Then one night the music stopped, and everybody looked to see why. And up there on the little stage behind the fancy new equipment they saw Uncle George breaking all the records, one by one, smashing them with his hands, and his eyes wild in his face."

She paused and looked down at the floor, then went on. "Well, they hustled him out of there and took him home to my aunt. Couple of times he tried to get hired on at other places, but he missed out. And Uncle George never did play the guitar again." Her voice had turned flat and hard, without the warmth Minerva had heard in it earlier. "When I was little I couldn't understand why. Now I do." She stood up abruptly and walked over to check the dryer.

Poor Uncle George, thought Minerva. What a sad story! And poor Mom. I didn't know she felt that bad.

Mrs. B. came in, and Minerva watched her absently as she shuffled along, her pink woolly slippers flopping at each step. Tonight she wore an enormous maroon dressing gown. Salvation Army special, Minerva guessed. She smiled and nodded as she passed, and Minerva heard a faint sloshing sound from the clothes hamper and the clink of coins in one sagging pocket.

With careful, almost delicate movements, Mrs. B. set the hamper down by the machine nearest Minerva and pulled out a purple bathmat and her awning dress. She took some coins from her pocket and fumbled two of them into the slot. A third fell to the cement floor and rolled to a stop at Minerva's feet. She picked it up and was about to give it back when she looked at it more closely. It wasn't a coin at all! It was a metal disc, silver-coloured, about the size of a quarter. Mrs. B. was ripping off the landlord! And getting away with it, thought Minerva, as she heard the muffled rush of water. Funny old Mrs. B. had actually outsmarted a complicated machine, had fooled it into doing what she wanted. For free. Minerva grinned.

"You know what they did?" Her mother sat down on the bench.

"Who?" asked Minerva.

"The store. They gave us all codes! Number codes, like a box of corn flakes! We're just part of the groceries now. That's what they think of us!"

"Well, Mom, it's like me having a password. It's a key. Does your code number open up your register?" Her mother nodded. "You see? It's nothing to get mad about."

"But Minerva, we have *secret* numbers, too,

numbers we're not supposed to tell anybody else, not even each other. It wasn't like that before. We never went around keeping secrets from one another! It's terrible!"

Minerva didn't know what to say. Right now she was feeling kind of terrible about computers herself.

"But that's not the worst," said her mother. "We just found out about this today. You know Elena? Kind of heavy? With dark hair?"

"The one who's so friendly?"

"Yes. The customers love her. But I guess the computer doesn't." Victoria Wright's face twisted in anger. "Elena got called in to the manager's office and bawled out for being too slow. You know how he could tell?"

Minerva shook her head.

"Because the computer knows our code numbers, so it can keep track of how many items we put across the scanner. Elena didn't have enough per hour, whatever enough is. The computer was spying on her! It's spying on all of us!"

"But Mom, it's...it's not really the computer that's spying. A computer just does what somebody tells it to do." That's the second time today I've said that, she thought.

"Then somebody better stop," said her mother. "Or there's going to be big trouble at Maple Leaf Supermarket." She got up and went again to the dryer.

Weird, mused Minerva. Almost funny, if you had a kinky sense of humour. The computer shafted both of us. And neither of us can do much about it. It wasn't right, she thought, and for the first time she saw that the computer could upset people, even hurt them. It was hard to admit it, because to her it had brought such certainty and joy. Strange how something could be both good and bad. But it wasn't the computer's fault, she reminded herself — it was the fault of the people who controlled the computer.

She joined her mother at the long table opposite the dryer and began to fold the laundry. Wish I could do something to make Mom feel better, she thought. There must be a way. There must be a way.

At the far end of the table Mrs. B. nodded and smiled at them again. Minerva smiled back, thinking of how Mrs. B. had outwitted the machine. If only Mom could do something like that... Suddenly she stood very still.

"Mom! There's a way!"

Victoria looked around, startled. "A way?"

"A way to stop the spying at the store!"

"How? Blow it up?" Her mother raised an eyebrow.

"No! By tricking the computer! Did you say it keeps track of the number of items for each cashier?"

"Yes."

"According to your code numbers?"

"Yes."

Minerva started to laugh. "Because that's how we can really mess everything up! Listen, Mom. Why don't you all switch codes? Every day you trade with somebody different!"

Victoria Wright looked shocked. "Minerva, we can't do that!" She glanced around as if someone might be listening and lowered her voice. "We're not even supposed to know anybody else's code, I told you that!"

"Why?" asked Minerva.

"Because... because..." Her mother stared at her in bewilderment. "I don't know," she said slowly.

"It's because they're afraid you'll do just what I'm telling you to do: use each other's codes. Then they couldn't keep track of your speed any more. Whoever programmed the store's computer fixed it so that when you punch in your code, it starts counting items for that code. Same with the other cashiers. But if you punch in somebody else's code, the computer doesn't know. A computer's really stupid, Mom. It'll just keep on counting items for that code, without knowing that the *person* is different. So, at the end of the week they'll have all their wonderful numbers — but they won't mean a darn thing! There's no way they can figure out who did what! It's beautiful!" Minerva laughed again. She felt better than she had all day.

"You sure about all that, Minerva?"

"Sure I'm sure."

Her mother grew thoughtful. "I don't know... It seems wrong somehow..."

"Is it right that you get spied on, that Elena gets bawled out for being friendly?"

"No-o."

"Well then?"

Her mother went on folding sheets, her movements brisk, almost angry. At last she spoke. "I can't, Min. It's too big a chance. If they found out they could fire me."

"Not if all of you do it together. Would they fire twelve experienced cashiers?"

"They just might!" said her mother. She snapped the wrinkles out of a towel. It sounded like the crack of a whip. "And we can't get by on Dad's pay. So there's no sense talking about it any more."

"But, Mom...!"

Victoria Wright picked up the folded clothes and started to walk towards the elevator. "I said there's no sense talking about it, Minerva! Forget it!"

"Okay, okay," muttered Minerva and continued the conversation in her head. Don't have to jump all over me, she thought, just because you're mad at the store. What you going to do then, just sit and mope like Uncle George? A fat lot of good it did him!

The elevator came and they got in. Besides, it's an absolutely brilliant idea, she thought. Now if only I could be that smart about my own problem... She glanced at the game program in her hand and felt sorry for herself. It would've been a good game. Maybe she could still work it out, even without a computer. She studied the last three lines.

```
90 ?"YOU HAVE DEDUCED THAT THERE ARE"

100 ?"THREE PEOPLE WITH THE OPPORTUNITY"
```

That was where she'd made the error. She read the lines again, and a strange excitement took hold of her. The words beckoned to her, teased her, seemed to promise her something.

Three people with the opportunity. Three people. Three people. Who had been in the computer room around ten after five, which was when Purcell said she'd changed her mark? She summoned the memory of the day before. She could almost smell the stale air in that cramped locker as she tried to recall what had happened.

Who had been there? Mr. Purcell. Rick, of course. And Barbara Fairfax. Three people. Three people with the opportunity to commit the crime.

The elevator stopped and Minerva nearly tripped as she hurried down the carpeted corridor, her thoughts churning. Hastily she put away the laundry that didn't need ironing and sat down at the little desk in her room.

She spread the paper flat. Okay. Purcell. Rick. Barbara. She wrote the names down and stared at them. Which one? And why? Why?

10

WHEN Minerva awakened the following morning the question was still with her. Why? And it stayed with her all through breakfast, through the slow journey to school on streets glazed with freezing rain, through math in homeroom, with Mr. Guthrie looking sadly at her every two minutes. And all during socials and family studies until lunch, when she sat down beside Sophie and asked, "Why, Soph?"

Sophie looked up from the last chapter of *Oliver Twist*. "Zed, perhaps?" she answered.

"No, you dope. Why did somebody change my mark?"

Sophie chewed thoughtfully on her tuna fish sandwich. "Not because they loved you, that's for sure." She took another bite and frowned in concentration. "Minerva, I think we have to look at it from another angle. Like, what happened because your mark was changed?"

"The end of civilization as we know it," said Minerva. "I'm not allowed in the computer room and I'm going steady with Pickle."

"Right. Now, Min, I don't want to hurt your feelings, but I can't believe Pickle's grooming you for the Olympics."

"Not unless they give medals for tripping."

Sophie grinned. "So, that leaves us with you being kicked out of the computer room."

"So," Minerva interrupted excitedly, "somebody wanted me out of there. And I've narrowed it down to three people, the only three who were there at the right time: Purcell, Rick, and Barbara." She looked puzzled. "But why would any of them want me out of there?"

"Well, there has to be a reason. Think, girl, think!"

"Couldn't be the student update..." mused Minerva. "I've done it for weeks now... Must have been something in that staff file..." She frowned at the table.

"Keep thinking. What did you see in the staff file?"

Minerva shrugged. "Pickle's old apartment number. Big deal! Who'd want to know that? Unless that's where she buries the bodies of kids who fail gym."

"What else?" prompted Sophie.

"Well, down one side there was a list of all the teachers' salaries."

They looked at each other.

"Salaries," Minerva whispered.

"That's it, Min," Sophie whispered back. "That has to be it! Now try to remember! Was there something weird about it?"

"Soph, I hardly saw it! As soon as I realized what file I got into, I figured I'd better get out fast!"

"Darn!"

The two of them sat silent for a minute, then Minerva said, "You know what we have to do, Soph?"

"I think I know, but I'm not sure I want to know," said Sophie.

"We have to get a copy of that list," said Minerva.

Sophie glanced around swiftly. "Don't talk so loud, Min!" She looked back at her friend. "How? You're not allowed near the computers."

"We'll break in."

"What you mean, 'we'?"

"Aw, Soph, you said you'd help!"

"I will, I will. I just have to get used to the idea of a life of crime. It wasn't my first career choice."

"Soph, it's not crime, it's detection!"

"Is that what we say to Purcell when we're caught?"

"One, we won't get caught. Two, what if Purcell's the crook?"

"You think he is, Min?"

Minerva frowned and shrugged. "Gee, I don't know, Soph. I only know he had the chance. Same with the others, except it's hard to believe it could be Rick, because he really stuck up for me in the office. Barbara's such a flake I guess anything's possible. And she lied about the earring. We have to see that file, it's the key to the whole thing. Which means I have to get into ODDSTARS..." Suddenly she groaned.

"Are you in pain?" asked Sophie.

"Yes," Minerva answered. "Purcell told Rick to make sure I couldn't get access. Which means he's probably killed my ID."

"Does that mean I don't have to buy burglar's tools?"

"Sorry, kid. It just means I'll have to use somebody else's password to fool the computer..." The same trick I told Mom to use, she thought, and laughed inwardly. "We need somebody who's got access to ODDSTARS, even if it's low level...somebody we can trust..."

Then both of them said at once, "Angelo!"

"You called?"

Startled, Minerva turned around. Angelo DeLuz stood behind her, his smile faintly wicked.

"You two look like you're planning the violent overthrow of the government."

Sophie and Minerva exchanged glances, then reached for Angelo and pulled him down to the bench between them.

"We are," said Minerva.

His wing-like eyebrows rose a fraction. "Is it a private revolution or can anyone join?"

"We're looking for one more very special person," said Minerva. "What we need is a guy with nerves of steel..."

"Check," said Angelo.

"...the courage of a lion," she continued.

"I don't need a night light any more."

Minerva nodded. "Good enough. The cunning of a fox..."

Angelo put on a crafty look. "I'm incredibly foxy, when you get to know me."

"...and access to ODDSTARS." She watched his face change.

"You've already got access, Min. Higher than mine, too."

"Not any more." Her mouth twisted a little. "They killed me."

"What? When? Why?"

"Taking your questions in order, I've been exiled from the computer room, yesterday, and why is what you can help us find out."

Angelo stared at her, all seriousness now. "I guess you better fill me in."

Minerva did, her voice trembling only a little, and when she finished he looked grim and angry. "Okay. You got a plan, Minerva?"

The bell rang. Minerva grabbed her tray and stood up with the others. "Can we meet after school?" she asked. "I mean after my heavy date with Pickle?" She made a face.

"Okay with me," said Sophie.

"I have to work today," said Angelo.

"We'll meet at the arcade, then. You're not busy every minute, are you?" asked Minerva.

"Gee, Min, I'm not supposed to go there," said

Sophie. "My father would freak." She looked worried for a moment, then brightened. "But he doesn't have to know, does he?"

Minerva laughed. "You've come a long way, Soph, baby! Okay, gang, synchronize your watches. It is now two minutes before thirteen hundred hours. At exactly 16:15 we meet at The Gamekeeper's behind *Robotron*. Over and out."

"Can I play a couple of games, Min? Please?"

"May I, James, you say 'may' when you're asking permission."

"Okay, okay, I'll say anything you want, man! Just answer me."

Minerva pulled her scarf tighter and hunched into her jacket. "Maybe one or two. But what if the Hulk's there?"

"I'll hide," said James. "Or run." He was silent for a moment, then asked, "How come we're even going?"

Minerva hesitated, not sure how much to tell him. "I have to talk to some people."

"Who?"

"Sophie and Angelo."

"Why?"

They turned into the shopping plaza. "Because," said Minerva.

"That's no sort of answer," James said scornfully.

"They're helping me with...with a project."

"Oh."

They got on the escalator. Minerva undid her jacket and dug some change from her jeans. She gave it to James.

"What kind of project?"

"Honest, James, I never met a kid who asked so many questions!"

"That's how you find out stuff. Mrs. Longo says I have an inquiring mind."

"She's right."

They stepped off the escalator and walked down the long hall to the bluish gloom of The Gamekeeper's. Minerva glanced around. Crowded as usual. She heard James take a quick breath beside her and felt him vanish into the shadows. Barbara lounged against one of the new laser-disc games, her T-shirt — a little too small, Minerva noted — scrawled with the voice-print warning off trespassers. Mark was close to her. Very close. In fact, he couldn't be much closer, Minerva thought. They looked like a two-headed mutant from one of the games. Struck by an impulse she couldn't resist, Minerva strolled over to them.

"Heard you lost an earring, Barbara. Did it ever turn up?"

With great reluctance, Barbara transferred her gaze from Mark's face to Minerva's, and the expression in her eyes changed from worship to something Minerva couldn't read. Was it suspicion? Guilt? Or simple bewilderment? It was hard to see much of anything behind the curtain of lashes, so thick they looked like spider legs.

The reply was slow and uncertain when it came. "I...I never lost an earring, Minerva."

If she didn't do it, thought Minerva, why is she acting so weird? She gave Barbara one of her top-quality cold stares. "Yeah?" she said, and then a sudden rage so filled her throat she couldn't speak. She turned and hurried towards *Robotron* at the back, and she could feel Barbara's eyes boring into her at every step.

Sophie stood deep in the shadows, peering suspiciously round the room. Minerva grinned. Probably thinks she'll be sold into white slavery any minute, she thought. Farther back, near the safety of the rear exit, James was hacking his way through an army of giant eggs in *Revenge of the Swampmaster*. Minerva caught a glimpse of Angelo threading his way toward them, the jingle of coins announcing his progress.

"Okay," she said when they were all together, "here's what I've got planned so far." She pulled a paper from her back pocket. "If you see any holes in it, interrupt." She smoothed out the sheet of foolscap, and the other two leaned towards her. "First, we've got to get into the computer room when nobody's there. Tomorrow night is the best time. It's Friday and the only night school is woodworking in the basement and English as a Second Language on the first floor. I checked the schedule. So the left front door of the school will be open from the outside until seven-thirty. Then they lock it. Soph, can you get out after supper?" Sophie's dad was really strict about her going out at night.

"Not if I tell the truth. Can't you just hear it? 'Dad, I have to go out for a while to break into the school. Is that okay?' So I'll say I'm going to the library." She thought for a moment, then said, "And it won't be a lie, I'll go. I need another Dickens fix. Finished *Oliver* today."

"Yeah? He die at the end?" asked Minerva.

"No, he inherits a pile of money. Most of the crooks die, though." Sophie's eyes lit up. "There's this really neat part, where Bill Sikes murders his girl friend, and then..."

"Okay, Soph, you can tell us later on..." began Minerva.

"...a crowd starts to chase him, and he slips off a roof and hangs himself, and then his dog, who's up on the roof, too, and who's the rottenest dog I've ever come across, tries to jump onto the dead body, but he misses and falls right down into a ditch and dashes out his brains!" said Sophie in a rush.

Minerva looked at her. "Soph, does your dad know you read stuff like that? Anyhow, I'm glad you can get out. It'll take me a while to find a way into the right file using Angelo's password, so I'll need a lookout." She turned to Angelo. "In fact, I'd like two. Ange, you don't have to come, you know, because all I need is your ID. So you can back out if you want to, but..."

Angelo bristled. "Back out? Have you forgotten you're talking to the guy with nerves of steel, the courage of a lion, and the cunning of a fox?" He drew himself up to his full height, just under Minerva's chin. "No way you can cut me out of the action, Minerva!" He looked smug. "Besides, no Angelo, no ID!"

Minerva grinned to cover the sudden lump in her throat. She'd been hoping he'd help, hoping she had another friend who believed in her that much. "You are pretty foxy, aren't you? Thanks, Angelo." She took a deep breath. "Is that it?" They nodded. "Okay, let's meet at quarter to seven at the Sir Ernest flagpole."

Sophie was frowning.

"What's the matter, Soph?" asked Minerva.

"I think I just found a hole."

"Where?"

"Um, well, won't the computer room be locked? Purcell's a complete psycho about that equipment."

Minerva groaned. "Aargh! And I'm supposed to be the logical one! How the heck are we going to get in?"

All three fell silent. Then a voice, a slow and ghostly voice, came out of the darkness. "Climb...the...wall... Climb...the...wall..."

Sophie's eyes got so wide they used up most of her face. Angelo's head nearly flew off his neck. But Minerva just said, "Okay, James, come on out!"

James peered out from behind *Swampmaster*. "Is it safe?"

"It's safe. Hofmann's gone. And I won't strangle you

till we get home. I want to give it my full attention."

James danced out, looked up at the three conspirators, and said, "You guys sure do neat projects. I can hardly wait till I'm in Pinevale."

"How much do you know, oh-little-brother-soon-to-die?"

"Everything." He smiled at them winningly. "Except why you want to break in."

Minerva sighed and explained. Again.

"You mean you were framed?" asked James.

He really watches too much TV, Minerva thought. "Yeah, I wuz framed, kid," she answered in a gangster's voice.

James was quiet for a few seconds, then he took his sister's hand and said, "You in trouble, Min?"

"Guess so." She smiled down at him.

"Then I'll help! I'll climb up and go through the window!"

"You out of your mind, James?" yelled Minerva. "All we need is for you to fall and break your neck!"

James pulled his hand away and stepped back, looking outraged. "Have I ever broken my neck? Even once?"

Minerva had to laugh. "No, not even once. But James, forget it, it's too hard and too dangerous!"

"Not for me! All you do is shinny up to the little roof over the door, swing onto a ledge, and grab the bar that holds the big floodlights. It's easy! Besides, I've already done it, remember?"

"I try not to," said Minerva with a grimace. She glanced at Sophie and Angelo. "Well, what do you think? Do we enlist Spiderman here on the side of justice?"

"Do we have a choice?" asked Sophie.

Minerva sighed again. "I guess not. Okay, James, you're in."

James beamed.

Minerva turned to Angelo. "Ange, can you make sure that the window nearest the floodlights is open a bit? Without anybody noticing?"

"No problem."

Sophie was frowning again.

"What's wrong now, Soph?" asked Minerva.

"Another hole, I think. Min, you and James'll be in the computer room, right?"

"Right."

"And I'll be hiding somewhere, and Ange'll be somewhere else, right?"

"Right. So?"

"So we'll be in three different places. How do we warn you if somebody's coming?"

"Right." Minerva scowled. "Never knew crime was so complicated. Ideas, anyone?"

"Walkie-talkies!" yelled James.

Minerva stared at him and then began to smile. "Daddy fix?"

"Daddy fix."

"We need three."

"I got two, Dad got one, two and one make three," said James.

Minerva's smile grew wider. "Brother James, I'm glad you're on my side."

She looked at the three of them. Sophie. Angelo. James. They were her friends. Her true and loyal friends. How could she ever have thought she didn't need them? She took a deep breath to steady her voice. "Okay, gang. That's it, I guess. Until tomorrow."

"Until tomorrow," they said.

11

MINERVA huddled into her jacket. The wind whirled a cloud of snowflakes at her, and she put her arms protectively around the plastic bag with the walkie-talkies. So far, so good, she thought. Dad had left at six, with a cake he'd just baked, to meet Mom at Aunt Lucina's birthday party way over in the west end. As soon as he closed the door, she found his walkie-talkie in the hall closet, James got his stuff together, they took the phone off the hook in case their parents called, and caught the twenty-after-six bus. Smooth as silk. No bugs. So far.

She looked at James. He was wearing running shoes, for the grip, he said, and old work gloves, on which he'd glued dots of rubber from his tire-patching kit. The coil of nylon clothesline round his waist made a yellow smear against his navy blue duffel coat, but the rest of him was lost in the darkness. When he did his Spiderman thing he'd be almost invisible.

A bus drew up, and two figures came toward them through the blowing snow. Sophie and Angelo. She pressed the tiny light button on her watch. It was dead on a quarter to seven. "Hi," she whispered.

"Hi," they whispered back.

"Why are we whispering?" whispered Angelo.

"Because we're master spies setting out on a perilous mission," whispered Sophie.

"Oh," whispered Angelo.

With Minerva leading, the gang of four moved like dark phantoms through the schoolyard to the grounds of Pinevale and melted into the shadows of the huge evergreens near the front door.

Light shone from the basement windows, where the woodworking shop was ready and waiting, from the main hall, and from the big room set aside for ESL on the first floor. The second floor was dark. Minerva felt for the little pencil flashlight in her pocket. Cars stopped nearby and disgorged their passengers, then pulled away to vanish in the snow. From the parking lot, in twos and threes and sixes, came a steady stream of students. Minerva motioned the others closer and gave out the walkie-talkies. James slid his into a pocket, with the flexible black antenna curling over the flap.

"We'll wait till there's a crowd going in, so nobody will notice," she said. "James?"

"Here, boss," he murmured.

"You ready?"

"Ready."

"Sophie?"

"Ready."

"Angelo?"

"Ready."

"Okay," whispered Minerva. "James, as soon as you're inside the room, send a message. Sophie, you stay underneath the window till you hear from us. We'll go in separately and take up our positions." Minerva heard herself talking and was amazed. Well, listen to me, she thought. You'd almost think I know what I'm doing.

She turned again to her brother. "James. Be careful."

"No sweat, Minnie. Remember you're dealing with Spidey."

Minerva lifted her hand, then flashed it downwards. "Go!" she whispered.

Deep in the dark of the pine trees, Minerva and Angelo waited. Angelo's face was hidden in the shadows, and all Minerva could see was one thin hand gripping the walkie-talkie. She chewed at her thumbnail, remembered, then chewed it anyway. If we get away with this, she promised herself, then I'll stop. For sure. Cross my heart and spit. As soon as Angelo's out of range, she thought, grinning.

The time crawled. She heard a mutter of static and tensed forward. Nothing. James must have reached the computer room by now! A tingle of fear touched her, receded, returned. "Is that thing working, Ange?" she murmured.

"Yeah, sure," said Angelo. He put it up to his ear. "I can hear somebody breathing."

Another crackle, and then a thin reedy voice. "Hey, anybody want a Frisbee?"

Minerva heard Sophie's muffled laugh, then she spoke into Angelo's walkie-talkie. "James, is that you? Where are you, for crying out loud?"

"I'm gettin' there... I'm on the little roof over the door... There's a whole bunch of Frisbees up here..." They heard a scraping sound, and Minerva's heart thudded. "I kicked them over the edge. Help yourself... Okay, I'm going the rest of the way...ledge is kinda slippery...over and out."

A click.

Sophie's voice.

"He's moving along the ledge... Going slow... there's ice on this side... He's just about at the floodlights. Oh no!" Her voice rose in a squeak of terror.

"Sophie!" Minerva grabbed Angelo's walkie-talkie with trembling hands. "Soph, what happened? Come in, Soph, come in!"

Sophie's voice, low and shaky, said, "It's okay, it's okay. He lost his grip for a sec. It's okay now. Sorry to scare you. He's reached the window, he's got one hand on the sill, I think...I can't see through the snow, just a minute..."

"Angelo, did you leave the window open?"

"'Course I did, Min. Stop worrying!"

"Can't help it. Wish we'd worked out every move on the computer first."

"You couldn't have. Too many human beings around to mess it up!"

"Spiderman here, come in, HQ."

"James! You okay?"

"A-OK, Minnie. Mission accomplished. Ow!!"

"What happened?"

"Walked into a chair. Just a sec till I get my flashlight... Okay. I see the door. I'll wait for your signal. Over."

"Roger. Okay. Time is now...nineteen hundred hours seven minutes. Sophie?"

"Check."

"Angelo?"

"Check."

"Remember, we go in one minute apart. Me first. No talk till you hear from me, unless there's trouble. Good luck!"

"Good luck, Min."

"Good luck."

Minerva stepped from under the tent-like branches of the huge pine and mingled with a crowd of students going through the door. Safely inside, she glanced up and down the corridor. No sign of Walter. Probably watching the hockey game in the basement. Let's hope he stays there, she thought.

Most of the crowd walked to the end of the hall and turned into the ESL class. Minerva hung back at the drinking fountain, bent to wet her mouth, and made a quick survey in both directions. No nosy teachers around. She saw Angelo and then Sophie come through the doors. Angelo headed up the front stairs, and Sophie walked nonchalantly towards her.

Minerva turned and ran up the back stairs. It was dark as a cave; she stopped and waited until she could see the vague bulk of lockers to her right, blacker than the surrounding black, and a grey smudge of window at the far end of the corridor. Then she ran silently to the door of the computer room.

She knocked once, then twice, the signal they'd agreed upon. The door opened immediately. She looked back the way she had come and flicked on her little penlight; Sophie answered, a brief flash. She looked towards the front stairs and repeated the signal; Angelo responded. She stepped into the room, made sure the door was locked, and let out her breath. So far, so good, she thought again.

"Hi, Min," James whispered. "Hey, is this place ever neat! Can I try one of the computers?"

· "*May* I, James." Minerva brushed past him to the terminal she'd been working on when everything came apart at the seams. Her heart was beating hard. She propped the penlight to illuminate the keyboard and let her hands rest on the keys. In the soft counterfeit twilight a great contentment spread through her. She felt as if a piece of herself, once lost, had now been found and fitted into place, and then thought suddenly of Uncle George, and of her mother.

She took the walkie-talkie from James and spoke

into it. "Minerva here. Starting up now." She switched on. There was the familiar low hum, and within seconds the screen glowed with green print.

"Can I, Min?"

"James, for crying out loud!" She glanced at his eager eyes, then relented. "Okay, sit down. Right beside me so I can keep an eye on you. This is our sound set-up. You want to see what your voice looks like?" She flipped on the power bar at the back and handed him the little mike. "You talk — quietly! — into that and your voice shows up on the screen. You press this bottom key to print it on the paper. Okay? Now don't bug me." She turned back to her own screen.

<pre>
        OXBRIDGE DISTRICT DATA STORAGE
             AND RETRIEVAL SYSTEM

                ODDSTARS Rev.2
</pre>

NAME?   ANGELO DELUZ, she typed.
PASSWORD? LUCIFER, she answered.
OK, said the monitor agreeably.

The prompt signal blinked at her. She sat back for a moment. Beside her she could hear James telling the computer he was really Spiderman.

Now it got hard. Angelo's access code was two levels below hers, so she'd have to trick the system somehow to get at the files she wanted. She depressed the walkie-talkie button again. "Minerva here. I'm into ODDSTARS, Angelo. Going to check what you can access. Stay tuned. Over."

She called up Angelo's files and watched them scroll up the screen in alphabetical order. Mostly test programs for his music stuff, and a couple of games. DTHMZGME. That was *Maze of Death*, a game he'd never finished. MUSICTST.1. MUSICTST.2. OCNDTST. That's *O Canada*, she thought. TSTQUEEN, whatever that meant. USER LIST.

User List. That'd be all the kids who could access ODDSTARS. Bet my name's gone, she thought sadly. Rick probably took it off. She asked for the file just to check. Names filled the screen. She stopped them at W.

It was there! Her name was still there! Rick didn't kill her! The job would be a snap now. "Hey, Ange, you there?" she whispered into the radio.

"Angelo here. What's up, Min?"

"My name's still on the user list! I can get in easy!"

"So do it, then. Sooner the better."

"What's the situation out there?"

"All clear at east stairs. So far," came Angelo's voice.

"All clear at west stairs," whispered Sophie.

"Okay, here I go. Logging off... Now back to sign-on..."

```
OXBRIDGE DISTRICT DATA STORAGE

AND RETRIEVAL SYSTEM

ODDSTARS Rev.2


NAME?

PASSWORD?
```

The screen waited. Carefully, her fingers slow and deliberate on the keys, Minerva typed in her name.

And the terminal went crazy. A fat green banner flashed on and off at split-second intervals. UNAUTHORIZED ENTRY! UNAUTHORIZED ENTRY! UNAUTHORIZED ENTRY! The words screamed at her silently. And then the machine began to howl, a long unending high-pitched beep that seemed to pierce Minerva's skull and plunged her into panic. For a helpless instant she was still, then her finger speared the RESET button. The howling stopped. The screen went blank, but in a moment, as if nothing at all had happened, it displayed the ODDSTARS sign-on and courteously asked for her name again.

She sat there trembling, her body clammy with sweat.

"What the heck was that?" Angelo's voice, higher than usual.

"Booby-trap," said Minerva shakily. "Somebody programmed an alarm to go off if I tried to get in." She took a deep breath in an effort to calm herself.

Back to square one, she thought. Can't use my own name. Her hands moved to the keyboard again, then stopped in mid-air. Why was the alarm triggered by her name? It was her *password* that gave her access, not her name... Maybe my password's still floating around in there somewhere... Maybe if I use Angelo's name and...

She leaned forward and started typing rapidly.

NAME?   ANGELO DELUZ

PASSWORD? LUCIFER

OK, said the screen.

I'm in, she thought. Now to try a little experiment. She keyed in CP, the command for changing passwords.

OLD PASSWORD? asked the monitor. LUCIFER, she answered.

NEW PASSWORD? Without hesitating Minerva typed FINGERS.

OK, said the screen.

The ODDSTARS sign-on routine came up. Minerva stared at it for a moment, and wiped the sudden sweat from her hands. She heard a buzzing and clicking beside her and glanced at James. Paper scrawled with inky peaks and troughs twitched out of his printer to fold itself into a pile on the floor. A thick pile. She remembered she hadn't shown him how to reset the playback to print just his own stuff, so he was getting all kinds of junk off the disk.

She turned back to her own machine. Now or never. NAME? ANGELO DELUZ, she replied.

PASSWORD? FINGERS. Minerva typed it in fast then closed her eyes and cringed, waiting for the alarm to go off. It didn't. She opened one eye and looked at the screen.

OK, it said.

Minerva laughed out loud. "Eureka!" she almost shouted. "Hey Soph, that's an old Greek word meaning 'Well, all *right*!' I'm in! Ange, I used your name and my

password. And it worked! Okay, now to find that file...
Over."

She pressed C and the complete catalogue of files
began to spill onto the monitor. In less than a minute
she'd found STAFFDOC.A and called it up. She thought
for a moment. She wasn't even sure what to look for.
She shrugged and hit the PRINT key. Might as well get
the whole thing and figure it out later, she thought.

There was a brief clacking, like a toy train switch-
ing tracks, and then the paper began to roll along its
twin tractors, filling up with line after line of print at
a hundred characters a second. Somewhere in that
mass of data was the clue, the answer, the way out of
the trouble she was in. She watched it grimly.

"Okay if I take the paper home, Min?"

"Huh? Oh, yeah, sure, James. Here, I'll rip it off
for..."

"Mayday! Mayday! Somebody's coming up the
stairs!"

"Ange, hide in the empty locker across from the
computer room! And keep reporting! Run!" She
gathered up James's paper and pushed it inside her
jacket, then doused both flashlights and hit the sound
system power bar. "James, get behind that filing
cabinet!"

She stood motionless, listening, poised for action.
Her printer chugged on. She leaned to look at it,
squinting in the darkness. Oh man, only up to the Gs!
How come the alphabet had so many letters anyway?

She heard a gasping sound, then Angelo's rough whisper. "Okay, I'm in the locker. It's Walter, I think. He's walking towards me. Stopping at every door."

"Angelo! Can you hear the printer with the walkie-talkie off?"

"All I can hear is my own heavy breathing, kid. Just a minute."

She peered at the printer again. Peters, Peterson, Quigley... Come on, you stupid machine!

"Min! Yeah, I can hear it, just a bit!"

Rossi, Ruznick, Santos, Sinclair...

"*Amor de Dios*, turn if off! He's almost here! Over and out!"

Minerva heard a click, then silence. She touched the ON LINE button and the printer obediently paused. She turned the monitor so that the screen was out of sight and dashed to flatten herself against the wall by the door. A pulse beat heavily in her throat, hard enough to hurt.

A key grated in the lock and the door opened. A ray of light sliced the darkness, bounced from the screens, roamed the walls. Minerva heard herself swallow and was certain the whole school heard it, too. She waited, all her senses sharpened by fear. Then the light withdrew, leaving the room darker than before, the door locked, and she heard footsteps receding down the hall. Still she didn't move.

"Min!" Sophie's voice. "He's coming toward me now. I'm going downstairs. Talk to you later."

Minerva felt her way to the printer and pushed the

ON LINE button again. Stark, Stevens, Strumpeter, Swoboda...

She flicked the walkie-talkie on. "Angelo, where are you?"

"In a locker slowly dying of oxygen starvation."

Minerva snickered. "You can come out now. I'm almost finished here." She glanced at the printer. Wilson, Worth, Yaremko...

"Red alert! Red alert!" Sophie's voice, urgent, staccato. "Purcell's here! Just came out of his office. Looking around...walking towards west stairs... Oh Lord bless me and save me! Out!"

Zimmer, Zuk...what kind of name was that?...Zylstra. Done! Minerva ripped the paper from the printer, sheets and sheets of it in a long ribbon. She shoved it into her jacket and turned off the machines.

"Min! Move it!" Angelo. "I'm in the main hall. Purcell's on his way up!" His voice cracked in alarm.

"James! Let's go! Plan Two!" They groped through the blackness to the window, and Minerva eased it up. James climbed out, tied his rope to the iron bracket holding the floodlights and slid to the ground. Minerva swung one leg over the sill and frantically reviewed what she knew about rope climbing. The only thing she remembered was "Don't panic," but it was too late now. She gritted her teeth, clambered out and grabbed the rope, then shoved the window down. It stopped at her right thigh. She'd left a leg inside. Can't go home without it, she thought. People might notice. Keys jingled at the door, and in a convulsion of fright she yanked her leg over the sill. She pulled the window shut and swung free on the rope just as the computer room was flooded with light.

Her heart thrummed like a sewing machine as she swayed to and fro. But as she inched downwards, the rope sliding through her leather mitts and her feet braced against the brick wall, she was filled with a fierce delight. Near the bottom she let go and landed in a snowbank. She lay back in it, her arms and legs outstretched and her faced turned to the sky. Thick flakes settled on her cheeks and mouth, and she shouted out loud, a fat and joyful sound that echoed in the night. "Eat your heart out, Nancy Drew! Minerva Wright has arrived!"

Sophie and Angelo came running around the corner of the school, their faces split with grins, and jumped into the snow with her. Angelo hugged her from one side and Sophie from the other, and both of them said, "You did it, Min, you did it!"

Minerva hugged them back. "*We* did it, you mean! No way it could've worked without you guys!"

"Yeah? What about me?" The voice came from above, and they looked up to see James on the little roof, rolling up his yellow clothesline. He slung it over one shoulder, then took a flying leap off the roof, to land on top of them in a tangle of arms and legs and laughing faces half-buried in the soft new snow.

Finally Minerva scrambled up, grabbed James and swung him aloft. "You too, Spiderman! You were terrific!" She held him close for a moment, and he squirmed to be let go, but his face was bright with pleasure.

The bus came then, in a cloud of steam and blue exhaust, and they ran for it. And it wasn't until Minerva slid gratefully into an empty seat that she realized she was soaked to the skin, tired all over, and happier than she'd been in a long, long time.

12

MINERVA scanned the list of teachers and consultants once more. Zilch. Zip. A big fat zero. Nothing suspicious at all. Maybe Sophie would spot something. She glanced at the clock on the stove. Almost one-thirty. Sophie should be here any time.

She got up from the kitchen table and moved to the stack of unfinished ironing. Yecch! Sheets. She hated sheets; they dragged on the floor and they wouldn't fit on the board and they never folded right, especially the fitted ones.

And why iron flat stuff anyway? Why iron anything? Just a waste of time. But her mother didn't think so. Not lately anyway. Minerva sighed and picked up the iron. Lately it seemed like her mom was out to win the Good Housekeeping Award of the Year. The place was so clean it was scary. Yesterday, on her day off, her mom had waxed all the floors, even under the rugs! Who looked under rugs? Weird. And she was on a real power trip, ordering the rest of them around like crazy. "James, put the bread away." "Minerva, turn off the bathroom light." "Greg, hang up your coat." Almost as if she had to control everything. Any day now we'll have to salute her, thought Minerva.

She finished one sheet and started another. And then felt mean. She knew why her mom was acting that way. She'd seen it before. Like that time when she was nine and Dad had lost his job and didn't get another for months. And last summer when James had climbed into a freight car and ended up in Detroit. Her mother had washed all the cupboards in the kitchen and cleaned out the junk drawer while she waited for the police to call. Whenever her mother was worried about something, something she couldn't control — SHA-ZAM! — she changed into Mrs. Clean-and-Picky. And right now it was the job thing that was bugging her. But this was one time when she *could* do something, thought Minerva. If she'd just trade codes, like they'd talked about... It was foolproof...

"Minerva, what in the dear Lord's name are you doing?" Her mother, dressed for work, ran into the kitchen and pulled the iron from Minerva's hand.

"Look!"

Minerva looked. A triangle of scorched material looked back at her, like a brand on a sheep. It was kind of a neat-looking pattern. "Sorry, Mom! Honest! I was thinking about..."

"Daydreaming more like! About that silly computer stuff of yours, I suppose!" She pointed at the pile of printouts on the table. "I'm sick of seeing it, I'm sick of hearing about it, I'm sick of thinking about it! It's a curse on the human race!" She was shouting now. "And now you've ruined that good sheet! Can a computer buy me a new sheet?"

Minerva flinched as if she'd been hit, and before she could stop herself she hit back. "You want a new sheet? I'll get you a new sheet! Stupid to iron them anyway! And besides, you're not mad about the sheet, you're mad about the store, and the secrets, and the spying, that's what you're mad at! Why don't you do something about it then, instead of yelling at me about a stupid sheet?"

Her voice started to tremble and she turned her face away. She suddenly felt like a scared little kid. Then her mother's arms were around her and even while she was looking down on the top of her mom's head, she still felt like a little kid. But not a scared little kid. Not scared at all.

"I'm sorry, Minerva."

"Me too, Mom. I didn't mean to say those things."

Her mother's body shook, and for an awful moment Minerva thought she was crying. She wasn't. She was laughing, a fine free laugh that Minerva hadn't heard in weeks.

"You didn't? Why not?" She smoothed Minerva's cheek with her hand. "We both know they're true." She stepped back, did up her coat, and grabbed her purse.

"And now it's time for me to go to work. See you tonight." She laughed again as she went out the door.

Minerva folded up the burnt sheet and was still trying to figure out her mother when the buzzer sounded. James reached the intercom ahead of her and spoke. "This is Crime Unlimited. Special rates on school break-ins, this week only. Password, please." She saw him grin. "Spiderman? Right on, Sophie. Come on up."

Sophie came in clutching a book, her finger acting as a bookmark. She'd probably been reading it all the way up in the elevator. Minerva glanced at it. Another Dickens. "*Our Mutual Friend*," Minerva read on the spine. Not what you'd call a catchy title.

"Well?" asked Sophie.

Minerva shoved the ironing board into the skinny closet beside the fridge, then sat down and opened up the long printout of the staff lists. "Nothing," she said. "I've been through it twice and I can't find a thing. You think it could be a fake name or something? We might have to look them all up in the phone book, which'll take forever."

"Let me have a look," said Sophie. "Maybe I'll see something you didn't."

"With pleasure!" said Minerva, and piled the sheets of paper in front of her. "I'll get us a Coke."

"What's this stuff, Min?"

Minerva looked around. "Oh, that's James's voice-print thing. Something about Spiderman. He wants to get it on a T-shirt this aft. Just put it on the counter."

She pulled the tabs on the Coke cans and sat down again. "Okay. How about if you take A to M, Soph, and I'll do N to Z. Then we'll switch, just to double-check."

They bent their heads over the endless lines of print, and there was no sound except the rustle of paper and the occasional sigh. Minerva yawned widely and noisily after she'd finished the Rs. She rubbed her eyes and leaned back in her chair.

Sophie looked up. "Sure makes for a dull story. No plot and too many characters." She yawned, too. "Find anything?"

"No." Minerva sounded disgusted. "And I don't think we will. What letter are you up to?"

"Just starting the Ds. You got any more Coke?"

"Yeah." Minerva got up and opened the fridge. She felt really low. She'd been so sure that the key was somehow in this file. Slowly she went through her own reasoning again, step by step, and couldn't find any mistakes. It *had* to be in this list! Nothing else made any sense. She slammed the fridge door savagely.

Sophie sat up with a jerk. "Well, well, well."

"What? What is it, Soph?"

"To coin a phrase, 'Eureka!' That's an old Greek word meaning 'Gotcha!'"

Minerva leaped up, and her chair fell over backwards. "Where?"

Sophie pointed. "Look."

Minerva read the name Sophie was pointing to, then stared blankly at her friend. "So?"

"So, that's it, Min! I know it is! Don't you recognize it?"

Minerva looked at the name again. "Dodger, Art F.," she murmured, then shrugged. "Should I?"

Sophie started to laugh. "Whoever it is has a great sense of humour. A little bent, but great."

"Sophie!"

"I always knew reading books would come in handy. Min, you know I just finished *Oliver Twist?*"

Minerva nodded. She looked grumpy.

"The best crook in Fagin's pickpocket gang is a boy named The Artful Dodger." She grinned up at Minerva. "Get it? Art F. Dodger!"

Minerva stared at the printout again, and slowly a smile spread over her features. "Soph, you're brilliant! No other word for it!"

"Sure there is," said Sophie. "There's smart, clever, brainy, gifted, keen, intelligent..."

Minerva ran into the living room and came back with the telephone book. She flipped to the Ds and began to move her finger down the columns.

"...bright, and quick-witted," Sophie was saying, "but generally I prefer to be called a mental giant. Minerva, why are you reading the telephone book, may I ask?"

"Doctura, Doda, Dodaro," muttered Minerva. "To see if Dodger's a real name... Dodd, Dodds, Dodgin..." She looked up. "No Dodger, Soph!"

"Only in Dickens' imagination, for which let us all be truly thankful!"

Minerva picked up the printout and peered at it. "A real rip-off artist, whoever it is. Two thousand bucks a month!"

"What's the address? Maybe we could stake it out!" Sophie's eyes lit up.

Minerva swore under her breath. "It's a box number. In Rexdale." She groaned. "That's way out in the west end. Takes half a day to get there." She let the printout fall. "How we going to catch him?"

"Or her."

"Or her," agreed Minerva. "But can you believe Barbara Fairfax reads Dickens?"

"I refuse to answer on the grounds that it may incriminate me. Last time we talked about Barbara we had a fight." Sophie grinned. "It is kind of far out, though."

Minerva glanced at the clock. "Come on. I told Angelo we'd be at the arcade by three. Besides, we could use another brain right now." She scooped up the lists and the voice-prints and packed them all in her knapsack. "James! Time to go! Bring money!"

Sophie checked out The Gamekeeper's and beckoned to them. Good. Mark wasn't there. James would live another day.

Minerva saw Barbara right away. She was hard to miss. She was wearing luminous purple harem pants with a hot pink T-shirt, and stretched across the front of the shirt was the spiky pattern of Mark's voice.

They found Angelo beside *Robotron* making change for the *Mad Planets* freak, who looked grouchier than ever. James dashed over to *Battle of the Time Lords*, stuck a quarter in the slot, and yelled "Credit!" to reserve the next play.

"Hi, Min, hi, Soph, what's happening?" said Angelo.

"Access your data bank, Ange," answered Minerva. "We need a plan." She pulled the lists from her knapsack and showed him what Sophie had found.

"So he zips out to Rexdale every payday and pulls a nice fat cheque out of his mailbox. Neat!" said Angelo.

"Which means he'll be going on Tuesday," said Sophie. "It's the end of the month."

Minerva stared at them, an idea slowly forming. "Hey, what if we write him a letter? We'll say we know who he is, and that we want a piece of the action. Then we set up a meeting and see who shows up..."

"That was on *Remington Steele* last week!" said Sophie. "One guy was trying to blackmail another guy..."

"Did it work?" asked Minerva.

"I don't know. My dad sent me to bed."

"That's a big help, Soph. Thanks a lot. Angelo? What do you think? The letter idea sound okay?"

James came running over to them. "I need more money, Min."

"Go away, James, we're really busy."

"But I need more money!"

"Why don't you go order your T-shirt instead?" She riffled through the paper till she found the voice-print sheets. "Here."

He took them and turned to go.

"How about this?" said Minerva. "'Dear Artful Dodger, We have figured out your scam and we want in.'"

"Sounds really pro," Angelo said. "But I don't think it'll work."

"Min." It was James again, pulling at her sleeve.

"James, for crying out loud, what is it?"

He held up the paper. "I don't know which is mine, the one that says 'I am Spiderman, Defender of the Helpless, Crusader for Justice' and stuff."

"Let me see." She flipped through the printout. "It's on the last three pages. See where the date and time are?" She pointed to the numbers "26/11 19:42" at the bottom, then tore off the pages and gave them to him.

"Why won't it work, Ange?"

"Well, if I were the crook, and I got a note like that, the first thing I'd do is wipe out all the evidence."

"Yeah, he'd be tipped off! That happened on *Hill Street Blues* once. LaRue set up a trap to catch this mobster, and..." Sophie's voice trailed off.

"And?" prompted Minerva.

"I didn't see the end of it. My dad sent me to bed."

Minerva gave her a look. "So you think he'd get back into the records, Ange? And kill off The Artful Dodger?"

Angelo nodded. "And then he wouldn't show up at

the meeting. We couldn't prove a thing, and we still wouldn't know who Art F. Dodger is."

"But the name's right on the printout!" Minerva waved the papers.

Angelo shrugged. "So? Who'd believe us? It'd be our word against his, and if it's Purcell..." He shrugged again.

"You have the makings of a fine criminal, Angelo," said Sophie.

"Thank you." Angelo bowed modestly. "I try harder."

"Shoot!" Minerva sighed in exasperation. "Now we're right back to square one." She frowned and let her gaze roam around the room. Suddenly her eyes widened, and she looked hard at Barbara. She shuffled through the papers in her hand till she came to the voice-prints, stared at them, and looked again at Barbara. Then she knelt down and spread the voice-print sheets on the floor.

"Bingo!" she said softly.

"I bet that's an old Jamaican word meaning 'Eureka!'" said Sophie.

"Right on, Soph! Have a look at this!"

A black patent leather high-heeled boot slammed down, just missing her hand. Minerva's eyes travelled upwards, past billow after billow of purple harem pants, to a hot pink T-shirt. There was a hot pink face on top of it.

"Are you trying to get my attention, Barbara?"

The face got pinker. "I'm trying to figure out what's

going down here! One, you ask me weird questions; two, you stare at me as if I'm Jabba the Hutt; three, you come on with the deep freeze every time you see me. I want to know why, Minerva!"

Sophie, half Barbara's size, took a step towards her and said, "Shove off, Fairfax, before I stomp on your eyelashes."

Minerva forced back a laugh. "Hold it, Soph." She stood up and eyed Barbara. "What does 'The Artful Dodger' mean to you, Barbara?"

"You kiddin'? It's a new wave band. They just made the charts with a hit single, *Brain Transplant*." She looked at Minerva incredulously. "Everybody knows that."

Minerva searched the other girl's face. It was a little angry still, but she could see no sign, no hint of deception.

"Okay," she said. "Two more weird questions, then I'll explain. First question: why did you sneak into the computer room around..." she bent to read something from the papers on the floor "...ten after five last Wednesday?"

Barbara stared at her. "Not that it's any of your business, but I forgot to turn off the sound system power bar after Mark — may he die a slow and painful death for standing me up today! — recorded his voice. I knew Purcell would foam at the mouth if he found out, so I hung around till nobody was there, then went in and turned it off." She folded her arms. "Anything wrong with that?"

"And then you told Purcell you'd lost an earring?"

"Yeah. How the heck do you know?"

"I was holed up in an empty locker across the hall."

Barbara blinked in surprise. "Well, whatever turns you on."

Minerva grinned. "Second question: did you say anything or make a noise when you turned off the switch?"

"Why would I do that? I was trying not to."

Minerva let her breath out in a long sigh. "Barbara, you're terrific!"

Barbara raised one eyebrow. "Can I have that in writing?"

"Any time!" Minerva picked up the sheets of paper.

"Wait a minute!" said Barbara. "The explanation, remember?"

"You haven't seen me in the computer room lately, right?" said Minerva.

"That's right. You been sick?"

Minerva smiled grimly. "In a way." She sketched in the events of the past four days, and ended with, "So you can see why we put you on our list of suspects. But now you've really helped."

Barbara was still shaking her head over what she'd been told. "Man, you sure got shafted! Who did it?"

"That's what we're trying to find out. Now we know it wasn't you, which leaves Purcell and Rick." Minerva folded up the sheets till the last one lay on top. "This may tell us. Look." The others crowded around her. "See, along the side here is the time, in one-second intervals, and this spiky line is the sound translated into print. Which is why Barbara can wear that jazzy T-shirt with Mark's voice all over it."

"May he die a slow and painful death," interjected Barbara.

Minerva flipped back to the beginning. "Here's Mark's voice. See how it matches the shirt?" They looked from the sheet to the shirt and back again. "That was recorded between 16:48:35 and 16:48:43, about ten to five on Wednesday." She turned a couple of pages. "Your stuff comes next, Angelo."

"What stuff?" he asked.

"Your own arrangement of *O Canada*, remember?" She held up several pages full of jagged lines all close together. "It triggered the command to record at, let's see, 16:53:08, and stopped at 16:53:37, when Purcell made you turn it down." She turned to the next sheet. "But here's where it gets interesting."

"You don't think *O Canada* was interesting?" asked Angelo, looking hurt again.

"Yeah, fascinating, Ange. Just a bit hard to sing," said Minerva. She laid the page flat on a nearby game. "Anyway, look at this."

They did. A row of wavy lines was scrawled lengthwise on the page. Underneath, on a horizontal axis, was the time it had been recorded. Minerva jabbed a finger at it. "Somebody said something at 17:07:52, something about five seconds long." She looked triumphantly at each of them. "Which is the exact time I was supposed to be fiddling with my gym mark."

"Then I snuck in and turned the switch off!" cried Barbara.

"Right," said Minerva. "And it wasn't on again till James fooled around with it the night we broke in. When he pressed the PRINT key, it printed everything from Mark's voice on, because that's where Barbara set the disk playback."

"So whoever said something at seven minutes after five is the slime who ripped you off!" yelled Sophie.

"Such language, Soph! Wash your mouth! Shame!" said Minerva.

"Slime is an old English word meaning slime," said Sophie.

Minerva turned to Angelo. "Ange, you're the sound man. We'd be able to hear those five seconds, wouldn't we?"

"Sure. It's part of the *Backtalk* program. It's all stored on the disk as electrical impulses, same as a record by *The Who* or *The Police*."

"Or *The Artful Dodger*," said Barbara.

"Terrific!" said Minerva. "Maybe we can arrange an audition." She looked at Barbara. "You want to help?"

Barbara was grinning like a little kid. "I thought you'd never ask," she said.

"Okay," said Minerva. "Here's what we'll do..."

Minerva's steps slowed as they passed the Maple Leaf Supermarket on their way out of the plaza. It was busy. Even the assistant manager was working for a change, giving out refunds for empty pop bottles. Minerva glanced down the row of cash desks, hoping for a glimpse of her mother. Not there. Strange. Maybe she was on her break. Minerva frowned a little, then her face cleared. Her mother was behind the snack bar, helping Elena.

She watched her mother take three hot dogs from the grill and hand them to a short man in denim overalls. He ate the first one in four bites and the second in three. Then, as Minerva stared in fascination, he shoved the third into his pocket, mustard and all, and shambled off.

When she looked back, her mother and Elena were deep in conversation. Their faces were serious. Then Elena nodded, grinned broadly, and nodded again, several times. Two customers arrived, and the women turned to serve them. Minerva caught her mother's eye and waved.

Her mother waved back, pointed to Elena, then to herself, then towards the cash desks, and switched the positions of three sugar bowls on the counter. She did it, thought Minerva, she's traded codes! She laughed and raised both arms in a victory salute. Her mother smiled at her, a slow sharing smile that had joy in it, and freedom, and something warm and strong and steadfast that Minerva knew would always be there for her.

Maybe Mom's found the part that was taken from her, the piece that was missing, she thought. Or

maybe even a piece that fits better than the old one.
And now she can be her own true self.

She waved once more and hurried to catch up to
James.

13

"ROPE?"

"Check."

"Tape?"

"Check."

"Watch?"

"Check." James held up his wrist.

"Okay, let's synchronize." Minerva looked at her own watch. "It's exactly...8:17:23."

"Minute fast." James pressed a button, then said, "Check."

The elevator arrived, and they got on. Their faces were grave with resolve as they rode down.

While they waited for the bus, jackets zipped tight against the cold wind, Minerva reviewed for the tenth time the plan they'd worked out in the last two days. She'd drawn a flowchart, with little boxes and circles and arrows showing the times and events, the paths to choose if something went wrong, and the result: catching the turkey who had messed up her life. And then she'd written a program, like the one she'd done before. The Minerva Program. Except this was for real.

And on paper it seemed perfect, even beautiful. First, because it was logical, with one act leading straight to the next. Second, because it was *right*. They were using the crook's own weapons to trap him. Minerva laughed inwardly as she climbed aboard the bus. It was so *right*.

Sophie beckoned from near the back. Minerva squeezed past the standing passengers, tripped over a tuba case, and fell into the seat.

"Hi, Soph."

"Hi. Ready for D-Day?"

Minerva lifted her eyebrows in a question.

"D for Dodger."

"I don't know. When we worked it all out it looked foolproof, but... If only I could have checked the whole thing on the computer!"

"Stop worrying! It's..." Sophie broke off, and her eyes widened. Minerva followed her gaze.

Barbara had just boarded. She was wearing a skin-tight silver leather jumpsuit with enormous orange zippers all over it, like sets of unbrushed teeth. Her hair, bleached platinum for the occasion, curved up from her head in dangerous-looking tusks. Minerva was awestruck. Barbara saw them and slowly lowered one bunch of eyelashes in a broad wink.

"Dear heart alive! Is she going to play sick in that?" whispered Sophie. "She looks like she's off to wrestle a shark."

Minerva laughed. "If she did, she'd win. Just be glad she's on our side." She shook her head in admiration. "You gotta give her A for guts, Soph. Can you imagine going to school in that outfit?"

"Surely you jest," answered Sophie. "I can't imagine getting out of my room in that outfit. My dad would lock me in without food or drink!"

The bus lumbered to a stop, and they all got out, James first as usual.

"James! Wait a sec!" yelled Minerva. She caught up to him. "Remember. Flagpole at 12:05. Got it?"

"Check, Min. See ya."

So far, so good, thought Minerva, as she slipped into her seat. She saw Angelo and waved him over. "Everything ready, Ange?"

"No sweat," he said in a low voice. "I rehearsed the whole routine yesterday. As soon as you come in... kapow! We zap him!"

O Canada filtered through the speaker in the corner, and they all stood. Minerva let her mind drift through the announcements, the morning reading, attendance. She spread the Program in front of her on the desk, her eyes focusing on the next instruction. "Line 60 — 9:55 MINERVA ASKS MR. GUTHRIE TO BE IN COMPUTER ROOM AT 16:05."

She glanced at him. He was at the blackboard writing. "SOURCES OF ENERGY," Minerva read. Right.

Day Three. She'd forgotten. Science first period.

Mr. Guthrie smiled down upon them. "Today we start a new...ah...a...new...um..."

"Unit, sir," someone at the front suggested.

"Yes, thank you, Mario, unit, yes, a new unit, of course." Mr. Guthrie smiled at them again. "There is a school of thought which holds that the history of the human...uh...the human..." He looked around the room, his brow furrowed.

"Being!" shouted a voice.

"Body!" shouted another.

Mr. Guthrie shook his head.

"Race!" said Minerva.

Mr. Guthrie's face cleared. "That's it, yes, race, thank you, Minerva." His glance stayed on her for a moment, and a look of concern temporarily banished his smile. "Now, as I was saying...what was I saying?"

Paula Carr raised her hand, stood up, and recited, "'There is a school of thought which holds that the history of the human race...' and that's as far as you got, sir."

"Ah! ...the history of the human race is also the history of the discovery and development of energy sources," Mr. Guthrie finished all in one rushing breath.

He turned back to the blackboard. "Now, let's see if we can make a list of different kinds of energy, ranking them from the simplest to the most complex. Any suggestions?"

"Coffee Crisp!" said Louie Fernandez. The class

laughed. Louie was as big around as a beach ball.

Mr. Guthrie started to write it on the board, but then stopped, smiled, and said kindly, "Well, Louie, of course you're right, as far as an individual human is concerned, but Coffee Crisp can't be used to drive a car or fly an airplane." He waited, chalk poised.

"Muscles," said Angelo.

"How would you know, DeLuz?" shouted Bill Rogers. "You only have one or two!" Some of the kids snickered, and Minerva gave them a dirty look.

"Yeah?" said Angelo. "At least mine aren't between my ears, jock!"

The class laughed louder. One for you, Angelo, Minerva said to herself. She grinned at him.

Mr. Guthrie tapped on the blackboard with his chalk. It broke in two. "Now, now, boys...quite right, Angelo. Muscle, both human and animal, was once — and for most of the world still is — the major source of...of..."

"Energy, sir." Several voices spoke in unison.

"To be sure," said Mr. Guthrie. He wrote "Muscle" on the blackboard. "Any other ideas?"

"Sun."

"Water."

"Steam."

Minerva tried to pay close attention, but once again her mind wandered back to the Program. It should work. It had to work!

"Coal."

"Oil."

"Gasoline."

"Nuclear energy."

Mr. Guthrie's chalk stub flew up and down the blackboard. Finally he turned, his face flushed and smiling. "Excellent, excellent!" He brushed his hands on his blue suit, leaving a trail of white dust, and put the chalk ends in his pocket. "Now, with each discovery of an energy source, human beings found new ways to make work easier. One can, in fact, view civilization as a process of making work easier. Perhaps we are a lazy species!" He laughed. Nobody else did. Except Paula. He cleared his throat and went on.

"When work changes, the way we live changes. Sometimes the changes are good and sometimes not so good. Let's take just one item on our list." He turned back to the blackboard and fumbled along the ledge. "Hmm...how odd! I was sure I had some chalk..."

"It's in your pocket, sir!" someone said in a loud whisper.

"Ah, yes, thank you," said Mr. Guthrie. He pulled out the chalk and drew a circle around the word "Gasoline."

"Gasoline is a high-energy fuel, that is to say, when it burns it can do a lot of work. It was a perfect fuel for the kind of engine that propels an automobile..."

Minerva tuned out again. Mr. Guthrie was good till the end of the period once he got going like this. She looked around. Half the class had glazed eyes. Mike Moncada was actually asleep, his head lolling forward on his chest. She looked at her watch. Twenty to ten.

Hope he stops early. Gotta talk to him — and Pickle will freak out if I'm late for family studies.

"...so while the car has been a blessing in many ways," Mr. Guthrie said, "its rise in the past century has meant the disappearance of the blacksmith, who made horseshoes, the saddler, who made harnesses and saddles, and the ostler, who looked after horses at roadside inns..." Minerva wondered idly what her dad would have been a hundred years ago. A watchman, she decided, one of those guys who walked around town ringing a bell in the middle of the night and yelling, "Two o'clock and all's well." Do that now and you'd be arrested, she thought. Probably her mom would still have worked in a store. But what about a hundred years from now, she mused, remembering her own vision. Or even fifty, or twenty? Would people even know what a cashier was?

"So with each step forward, that is to say, each time work is made easier through a new...a new..." He stopped again, bewildered. Paula jumped up and prompted him.

"Thank you, Paula."

Paula smirked and settled herself importantly in her front seat.

"As I was saying, each step forward, each change, brings with it many changes we cannot foresee, changes that can cause hardship. It's up to all of us to ensure that there is as little hardship as possible." He looked around the room in a bemused fashion. "That is part of our responsibility as scientists and as human beings. Thank you." He bowed.

Minerva smiled a bit as she gathered up her notebooks. She was almost sure Mr. Guthrie had forgotten where he was and had given a speech he'd made some place else. Most teachers didn't bow at the end of the class. What a character! Nice. But weird, man, weird!

She approached his desk. The other kids had gone, except for Angelo, who was hanging around outside the door.

"Sir?"

"Yes, Minerva?" He smiled.

Off to a good start, thought Minerva. "Sir, are you busy after school?"

"Well, now, let me see...I believe I said I'd drop in on the chess club...is today Wednesday?"

"No, sir, it's Tuesday."

"How odd! I could have sworn..." He stared at his desk calendar.

Minerva started to get edgy. "Sir?"

"Yes, Minerva?"

"About after school?"

"Would you like to see me?"

Minerva plunged in. "Yes, sir, I would. I'd like you to come to the computer room at five after four."

"The computer room? But I thought..."

"That I'd been kicked out? Yes, but sir, I never did what they said, and now I've got proof that somebody else fooled with my marks, and I want you to be there as a witness." She stopped, out of breath. "Please, sir?"

He stared at her, his face serious. "Minerva, are you sure you know what you're doing?"

Her chin lifted a little. "Yes," she said. "Sir."

He stared at her some more, then began to smile, that sweet smile of his that always made you want to smile back. "I'll be there, Minerva. It will give me great pleasure."

"Sir, uh, just to make sure, will you mark it down on your calendar?" She pointed at the open page.

Mr. Guthrie chuckled and looked around for a pencil. Minerva gave him one.

"Okay, sir, thanks! Remember, five after four!"

She ran out the door, gave the V sign to Angelo, and took off for family studies. On the way she pulled out the Program and put a check mark beside Line 60.

Line 70 — 11:45 SOPHIE AND MINERVA LIBERATE VOLLEYBALL NET. The instruction seemed burned into her memory. This was where things got risky.

Two minutes to go. Minerva swung over the padded horse in the gym and glanced at Sophie, who nodded imperceptibly.

"Very good, Wright," said Miss Dill. "Much better."

Minerva's mouth dropped open in shock. "Pardon, Miss Dill?"

"I said you're doing much better, Wright." Miss Dill smiled. "Those extra hours are paying off already, you see."

Minerva closed her mouth and tried smiling back. It wasn't as hard as she thought. She lined up with the others against the wall and edged nearer Sophie.

"Move over, Nadia Comaneci!" whispered Sophie.

Minerva snorted. "Can you believe that? Pickle actually praised me!" She looked again at Miss Dill. "You know, Soph, when she smiles she's almost humanoid."

"You *are* getting better, Min."

"I am?"

"Yep. Not a heck of a lot. But at least your legs act as if they're part of the rest of you."

"No kiddin'?" Minerva felt obscurely pleased. Not that I care about gym, she thought. Just that it's sort of a hassle being a klutz.

The whistle shrilled and fell from Pickle's mouth. "All right, girls, put away the equipment!"

Sophie turned to Minerva. "Now?" she whispered.

"Now," answered Minerva.

It was a quarter to twelve. They mingled with the others. Each picked up a mat and carried it into the little supply room off the gym. Sophie slipped to the back and curled her small body behind a storage chest. Minerva stacked up the mats with great care, her eyes darting this way and that until all the girls had left. She pulled a garbage bag from under her gym suit and dropped it on top of Sophie. Then she opened the storage chest and lifted out a volleyball net. It joined the garbage bag.

"Okay, Soph?"

"Uh-huh. Just keep watch. If we're caught we'll get a year of detentions!"

"Never fear, Minerva's here!" She moved to the door of the supply room and peeked into the gym. Empty. "Okay, Soph!" Behind her she could hear the rustling of the plastic bag as Sophie stuffed it full of volleyball net. The noise seemed loud in the silent room. She glanced to her right and left. All clear. Then across the gym she spotted the familiar green jogging suit. She slipped back inside and whispered, "Danger!" The rustling stopped.

She waited, tense and sweating, for a sound from the gym. Nothing. Cautiously she moved her head so she could see with one eye. Pickle was still there, standing alone by the window. Except it didn't look like Pickle. The straight shoulders were slumped now, her head was bent, and her face, usually as tough and secret as a stone, was all soft and opened up. Minerva blinked and looked again. Was it possible that another Pickle was hiding inside the green jogging suit? That right now she was seeing the real Pickle? For a moment Minerva felt almost friendly towards her.

Then, as she watched, Miss Dill snapped to attention and her face closed up. She did five quick knee-bends and strode out of the gym.

"Min! You still there?"

"Right here, Soph! All clear now! Pickle's gone!"

Sophie crawled out from behind the chest. Minerva glanced at her watch. Five to twelve.

They threw on their clothes, dashed across the hall to

get their jackets from the washroom, and hurried through the lunchtime crowd to the schoolyard next door. Minerva carried the garbage bag.

James was waiting at the flagpole. Minerva handed him the bag. "Here it is, James. Can you get it fixed up by four?"

"No problem, Min."

"Okay. Be careful!"

He waved.

Minerva drew the Program from her pocket and put a tick beside "Line 80 — 12:05 MEET JAMES AT FLAGPOLE."

The afternoon dragged. Minerva frowned at the clock in the resource centre, where she was supposed to be doing a book report. Twenty after three. Forty more minutes, she thought, and her stomach tightened.

She pulled out the Program and read through the last part of it again. No bugs so far, but that didn't mean a thing. It could crash any time. She chewed at her thumbnail and watched the clock hobble towards the half hour. The bell rang. At last. She ran to her locker.

Pickle wasn't in the gym. She's got to show up, thought Minerva, or the Program won't work. She plucked a basketball from the box in the corner and flipped it towards the net. It went through cleanly. Very good, Wright, she said to herself. She stepped further back until she was nearly at the centre line, took aim, and sent the ball aloft. Once again it sped true to its target. She moved to the sideline, where the angle of play was close to forty-five degrees, crouched, and threw. The ball arced gracefully in the air and plunged through the net. "Right on, Wright!" she whispered.

She grabbed the ball on its first bounce and ran softly back beyond the centre line to the far end of the court. "And now, fans," she murmured, "with the score tied and only seconds left to play, Minerva Wright, known to her teammates as The Sniper, has intercepted a pass deep in her own territory. Will she go for it? It's an impossible shot, ladies and gentlemen, but The Sniper is famous for doing the impossible. She's taking aim, and..."

Minerva hurled the ball the full length of the court. It grazed the backboard, wobbled, spun dizzily around the steel rim of the net, settled, and fell through. "Wright has won the game for Pinevale, ladies and gentlemen, with an utterly incredible shot..."

Minerva broke off, startled, as applause reached her ears. She turned to see Miss Dill at the door of the gym. Clapping. And smiling. Sort of. Minerva felt foolish and wondered how long Pickle had been standing there.

"Wonderful shots, Wright!" Pickle moved towards her. "Why don't you play that way in class?"

Minerva didn't know why she told Pickle the truth. She never had before. "Because I'm a born klutz, Miss

Dill. When anybody watches me, I get all confused and nervous. And I trip. Or fall. Or do something dumb. Then when they laugh I just get worse." As if to prove it, she bounced the ball clumsily and it got away from her.

Miss Dill snared it neatly with one hand. "Nobody is a born klutz, Wright. It's just a matter of mental discipline. Physical excellence means mental effort. Forget about how you look, forget about other people and what they think! Concentrate on your goal! It's the only way!"

She fell silent. Minerva stole a look at her and almost wished she hadn't, for she saw again the Miss Dill she'd seen that morning. Man, you can't trust anybody these days, she thought. Here I had Pickle all figured out as one hundred percent pure mean...

"Mental discipline, Wright!" Pickle said again. "Now. Let's try it, shall we? Your goal is to score. My goal is to stop you." She flipped the ball to Minerva and took up a guard's stance. "Pretend I'm not here, Wright. And concentrate! Concentrate!"

She's gotta be kidding, thought Minerva, as Miss Dill flailed the air between them like a green octopus. Her arms were everywhere at once. Minerva concentrated on concentrating. She took a step, bounced the ball, retrieved it. She did it again, faster. Then, surprising herself most of all, she whirled, took another stride, then leaped into the air above Pickle's outstretched arms and fired the ball towards the basket. She knew it was dead certain as soon as it left her hands. The ball sailed through the net and fell with a satisfying *thunk* to the floor below.

"Excellent! Excellent!" Pickle scooped up the ball and turned. The smile was back. "I'll make an athlete out of you yet, Minerva!"

Minerva? Since when Minerva? thought Minerva. Does this mean I should call her Hildegarde? Before she could make up her mind, Sophie appeared at the door.

"Miss Dill! Miss Dill!"

Minerva looked at her watch. Three minutes to four. Right on time.

"What is it, Michaloff?"

"Mr. Purcell wants you right away! In the computer room! Barbara Fairfax is unconscious!"

Very good, Sophie, thought Minerva. Convincing. I believe you myself — and I wrote the script. She took the Program from the bench on her way out and checked off "Line 90 — 15:57 SOPHIE GETS PICKLE." Then she followed Miss Dill upstairs.

The moment of truth had arrived.

14

MINERVA paused at the door of the computer room and counted heads. Purcell, Guthrie, Dill, Angelo, Rick, Barbara, Sophie ...all here. She stepped across the hall and tapped twice, softly, on a locker. Two answering taps came back to her. Good. James was ready.

She walked into the room and closed the door. The scene of the crime, she thought. Just like in a mystery story. All the main characters gathered together while the brilliant detective unravels the plot.

Barbara was still doing her thing, stretched out on the floor with her eyes closed as if she'd just been sacrificed. Miss Dill was kneeling beside her. Purcell and Guthrie looked worried. Sophie pretended to look worried. Rick was eating corn chips and frowning at a terminal. And Angelo sat in front of the sound micro, one hand on a pile of papers, the other near the power bar. Minerva glanced at him. He nodded.

Here goes, she thought. Line 100 — 16:05 THE TRAP IS SPRUNG.

"Okay, Barbara, you can get up now."

For a moment Minerva felt like one of those faith healers Aunt Lucina watched on TV, as Barbara, in one fluid silver movement, rose to her feet.

Mr. Purcell was the first to find his voice.

"What is the meaning of this charade, Miss Wright?" His words were like chipped ice, and Minerva almost lost her courage. Then she remembered what she knew.

"Sir, I told you — all of you — that I didn't change my mark. Now I've got proof. And I want all of you to hear it."

She saw Rick turn around slowly and stare at her. The bag of chips crackled in the silence. Mr. Guthrie stood near the door, his eyes bright with friendliness. Miss Dill, beside him, looked puzzled.

"We've already had proof enough, Miss Wright," said Mr. Purcell. "And quite enough of your insolent theatrics, too. I want all students out of here immediately! This is absurd!"

"Just a minute, Peter," said Mr. Guthrie. "I think we should listen to her."

"I agree." It was Pickle! Minerva couldn't believe her ears. "Give the girl a chance, Mr. Purcell," she was saying. A strange smile crossed her face. "After all, you're a fair-minded man, aren't you?"

Mr. Guthrie chuckled. Then he and Miss Dill smiled at each other as if they'd just been given a present.

Purcell looked narrowly at both of them. "I hope I am known to be and seen to be, Miss Dill," he said stiffly. "Very well, Miss Wright, you may proceed."

"Thank you, sir." Minerva took a deep breath. "You all remember that I got into a staff file."

Nods and frowns.

"Well, it didn't take long to figure out that somebody didn't want me to see something in that file. That person fixed things — changed my phys. ed. mark — so I'd be barred from the computer room." She had their full attention now. Even Rick, still methodically eating corn chips, leaned forward with interest.

"The first thing I had to do was get a hard copy of that file. Which meant breaking into the computer room, and I'm sorry about that, sir, but it was the only way." Mr. Purcell was frowning again.

"The next thing was getting past the booby-trap in the system. That was yours, Rick?" He nodded and she smiled. "You goofed. In fact, you actually helped. You should have blocked me at the password level. All I did was change Angelo's password to mine, and I got right in."

"Clever of you." Rick scowled. He looked as if he could kick himself.

"Thanks," said Minerva. She hurried on. "Anyway, I got the printout of the file. But I couldn't see anything weird about it. It was my literary friend here who spotted it. Soph?"

Sophie stepped forward and held up a page of the printout. "I'm into Dickens this term. So when I came across this" — she pointed to a name circled in red — "I knew it was a phony. 'Dodger, Art F.' just had to be The Artful Dodger from *Oliver Twist*."

Minerva took the page from her. "And this Artful Dodger was picking pockets, too. He was sending himself two thousand dollars every month."

"Impossible!" Mr. Purcell exploded. "Young lady, how do we know you haven't made all this up? I warn you..."

"Oh, hush up, Peter!" said Miss Dill.

Purcell's mouth opened and shut like a beached fish. He hushed up.

Minerva went on. "But we still had no way of catching him. The address in the file was a post office box out in Rexdale. If it hadn't been for Barbara's T-shirt...Barbara?"

Barbara sauntered to the middle of the room, and slowly, almost as if she were doing it to music, unzipped all the zippers in the top of her silver jumpsuit. Here. There. Across. Down. Under. Behind. Around. Minerva heard Angelo gasp, and Purcell's eyes bulged in alarm. The top hung for a moment, then fell away, to reveal the hot pink T-shirt with spiky lines.

"What you see there, apart from, uh, quite a bit of Barbara, is a print of Mark Hofmann's voice, made at about ten to five the day I got into the files. Angelo?"

Angelo pressed some keys and turned the volume

knob. From the speaker nearby came Mark's voice, thin, raspy, but recognizable: "Hands off. Trespassers will be boiled in oil. Property of Mark Hofmann."

"May he die a slow and painful death," muttered Barbara.

Minerva held up a sheet of paper next to Barbara's chest. "This is a printout from the disk you just heard. You see? It matches."

Eyes looked back and forth, heads nodded. Rick finished off his chips, crumpled the bag, and pitched it into a wastepaper basket. He yawned.

"Mr. Purcell, sir, you came in around that time with my little brother James. And while you were yelling at me, Barbara and Mark snuck out. But Barbara forgot to turn off the switch on the power bar. So the next thing that was recorded, at seven minutes to five, was ...well, I'm sure you'll remember it." She turned to Angelo. "Maestro?"

Angelo pressed keys again. A long mournful howl filled the room, followed by a cluster of terrible screams, and then the clash and scrape of metal on metal. Purcell clapped his hands to his ears, and Miss Dill's jogging suit jogged all on its own. Mr. Guthrie put a calming hand on her arm.

"Okay, Angelo," said Minerva. She looked at him. He hadn't heard her. "Okay, Angelo! That's enough! Ange!" she yelled. He came to and flicked off the switch.

"That was *O Canada*, arranged by Angelo DeLuz," Minerva said. "You do remember it, sir?"

"Once heard, it's hard to forget, Miss Wright," answered Mr. Purcell.

"Nothing else got recorded until" — Minerva glanced at the papers in her hand, just to be absolutely sure — "seven minutes and fifty-two seconds after five o'clock that day." She stopped and looked around the room. No one said anything. "Which was exactly the time I was supposed to be changing my phys. ed. mark."

All at once the air was charged with tension, and Minerva's skin prickled. Sounds came to her magnified: the hum of Angelo's computer grew loud as a dentist drill, her own breathing seemed like waves on rocks, and she was sure she could hear the click of tiny muscles when Rick blinked his watchful eyes.

"So..." she paused to steady the sudden shaking in her legs — "the next voice you hear belongs to the person who committed the crime." She gestured to Angelo.

She watched as Angelo's hand moved to the keyboard and pressed a key, moved to the volume control and turned the knob. Then sharp and shocking in the waiting silence of the room came the sounds. A loud crackling, like paper being crumpled, a chewing noise, and then a voice, known to them all: "The Artful Dodger strikes again!"

As if pulled by one string, their heads turned, and they stared at the owner of the voice. He walked towards them, unhurried, an odd little smile on his face.

"Congratulations, Minerva."

"Thanks, Rick." Her voice broke on his name, and she felt half angry, half sad, that it had to end this way.

Rick shrugged one shoulder. "Sorry you got caught in the works, kid."

"Sorry?! Sorry?!" Sophie lunged at him. "Is that all you can say? After what you did to my friend?" She punched him in the stomach. "You maggoty scoundrel! You two-faced knave! You...you limb of Satan!" She punched him again. "You hog's breath!"

I think she's upset, thought Minerva. She grabbed Sophie and held her back.

Rick shrugged again and turned to Mr. Purcell.

"Does this mean I'm fired, Uncle Pete?"

Minerva looked at the principal and was sure he would self-destruct before their very eyes. His face was the colour of a ripe plum, and his hands were so tightly clenched she was afraid he'd break his own knuckles. He opened his mouth several times, but no sounds came out. Finally he managed a squeak.

"How much?"

Rick stuck his hands in his pockets and hitched up his pants. "Not a heck of a lot. Six thou. It was a tidy little scam for a while." He looked around at everyone. "Hey, you don't think I did it for the money, do you? That was just icing on the cake. I wanted to outsmart the system, that's all. It wasn't hard. You've got a real Mickey Mouse set-up, Uncle Pete."

Purcell pointed at a chair, then at Rick. "You ...sit ...down...over...there. Don't move. I'm going to talk to the Board immediately." He turned and ran to the door.

Oh, no, thought Minerva. "Just a minute, sir! Wait! Stop running..."

It was too late. A terrified squeal came from outside the door.

The Minerva Program had worked. Right down to the last line, she thought. "JAMES DROPS NET ON FIRST PERSON TO RUN OUT OF COMPUTER ROOM." Mr. Purcell was all tangled up in the volleyball net she and Sophie had swiped. James had dropped it, as instructed, and then pulled the drawstring tight. Mr. Purcell was clawing at the tough black string and making little mewing sounds.

Minerva could hear Sophie and Angelo and Barbara shouting with laughter behind her. Miss Dill and Mr. Guthrie came out to the hall, took one look, and started to laugh so hard they had to hold each other up.

She stared at poor Mr. Purcell. Wonder where I went wrong, she thought. She pulled out the pages of The Minerva Program, their foolproof plan. She had worked it all out so *logically*, step by step by step. It had seemed perfect. No bugs. No glitches.

But there was poor innocent Mr. Purcell squirming on the floor in front of her. Her glance travelled down the lines of statements. She frowned. Then her face cleared and she walked over to Mr. Purcell and sat down beside him.

"Miss Wright," he said hoarsely.

"Yes, sir."

"Do you have an explanation for this?" His eyes looked all wobbly, as if they'd come loose.

"Yes, sir, it's right here. See? Line 200? Well, that's where I should have set up an IF...THEN statement, and then probably a couple of subroutines..."

"Get me out of here!" roared Mr. Purcell.

Minerva thought about it for a moment, then moved to release him.

It was, she decided, the logical thing to do.

EPILOGUE

HI. This is Minerva speaking. A lot of neat things have happened since the day of The Minerva Program, and I thought you'd like to hear about them.

I'm back in the computer room, of course. As a matter of fact, I help the younger kids with programming. So does Mr. Guthrie, when he remembers, and Mrs. Sinclair, at least until she takes over as principal in the fall. Which we're all pretty happy about.

Mr. Purcell? Would you believe he got a promotion? He's going to be in charge of something at the Board. Probably money.

Rick wasn't put in jail or anything. But he had to work for six months over at ODDSTARS without getting paid. While he was there he made up a new video game called *Fourth Dimension* and now he's getting rich. Fast. Who says crime doesn't pay?

When the bosses at Mom's store finally figured out how the cashiers had messed up all their beautiful numbers they didn't know what to do. So Mom told them: she made them promise to get the central computer reprogrammed so it doesn't spy any more. She's a lot happier, too. I can tell because the floors need waxing and the junk drawer's filled right up again. And Dad only works part time at the hospital now. The rest of the time he's a cook, a real cook, at Sophie's uncle's restaurant on the Danforth. When Mom works nights, James and I go down there and have our supper with him. Unless it's fish.

We hardly ever call Miss Dill "Pickle" any more. First, because she went out and bought some new jogging suits that aren't green, they're yellow and purple. (Sophie said we could call her "Banana" or "Eggplant," but it didn't seem as much fun.) Second, because she's not as sour as she used to be. In fact, she's really not too bad. She even gave me a 65 in phys. ed. this term, and she lets me play sub on the basketball team. (By the way, remember that new address? It's the same as Mr. Guthrie's. Interesting, huh?)

Angelo got to play his computerized version of O Canada at the Christmas concert. Only seven people left. And three actually clapped. I think they were just glad it was over. Now he's working on God Save The Queen. By the time he's through she'll need all the help she can get.

Barbara's letting her hair grow normal — it's brown and down to her earlobes now — and she's hanging out

Some other Puffins

THE SEVENTEENTH SWAP
Eloise McGraw

$17.99 is a huge amount of money to find when you only own three things in the whole world. But the outline of a brilliant scheme begins to form in the mind of twelve-year-old Eric Greene — The Great Double Multiple Swap! He begins his race against time to organize a complex series of swaps starting with a triangle stamp and ending with . . . the red and black cowboy boots? Maybe, if only he can fit the pieces in the jigsaw together in time . . .

RAGS AND RICHES
Joan Lingard

When Sam and Seb's mother discovers a coat lined with a thousand pounds in her own second-hand clothes shop, she doesn't know what to do. But money isn't their only problem. There's Granny who falls in and out of love with a butcher, and then there's the saga of Seb's heart-throb, Viola. Will he ever ask her out? An entertaining book by a supreme storyteller.

BIKE HUNT
Hugh Galt

When Niall Quinn's brand-new racing bike is stolen, he becomes over-keen to track down the thief and finds himself involved in rescuing a kidnap victim hunted by gunmen. Lost in the mountains and in great danger, he realizes that Katy, his logical, brainy friend, is the only one who knows how to find him.

BOSS OF THE POOL
Robin Klein

The last thing Shelley wanted was to have to spend her evenings at the hostel where her mother worked, because she wasn't allowed to stay in the house on her own. Then, to her horror, mentally-handicapped Ben attaches himself to her and although he's terrified of the pool, he comes to watch her swimming. Despite herself, Shelley begins to help him overcome his fear. A compassionate story of the growth of an unlikely friendship.

MATILDA
Roald Dahl

Matilda is an extraordinary girl, sensitive and brilliant. But her parents are gormless, and think Matilda is just a nuisance and treat her as a scab, to be endured until the time comes to flick her away. As if this isn't enough, she has to cope with the odious headmistress, Miss Trunchbull. When Matilda is attacked by Miss Trunchbull one day, she suddenly discovers she has an extraordinary power which can make trouble for the monstrous grown-ups in her life.

NOW THEN, CHARLIE ROBINSON
Sylvia Woods

Charlie Robinson is always full of ideas, whether he's trying to liven up a maths lesson, solve the mystry of noises up a chimney or turn the Nativity Play into a really special event. His exploits at home, at school and out and about in the village make very entertaining reading.

TORCH
Jill Paton Walsh

Dio and Cal had gone to ask the old man for permission to marry. Instead, Dio finds himself commanded to be the Guardian of the Torch in the old man's stead. Without quite knowing why, they embark on an extraordinary journey bearing the Torch in search of the Games! In doing so, they learn some of the secrets of the Torch and of the mysterious past time called 'Ago', a time of wonderful machines, now lost for ever.

THE THIEF
Jan Needle

Poor Kevin hasn't got much going for him at the moment. The only interest he has in life are the caverns — the dangerous, derelict caverns which stretch for miles beneath the woodland by the town. The caverns become Kevin's refuge and obsession. He goes exploring and one day discovers a stash of stolen goods, and this is when the real nightmare begins.

CRUMMY MUMMY AND ME
Anne Fine

How woud you feel if your mother had royal-blue hair and wore lavender fishnet tights? It's not easy for Minna being the only sensible one in the family, even though she's used to her mum's weird clothes and eccentric behaviour. But then the whole family are a bit unusual and their exploits make highly entertaining reading.

THE BEWITCHING OF
ALISON ALLBRIGHT
Alan Davidson

Alison has always sought refuge in day-dreams: of a lovely home, of being an exciting person, of doing all that the others at school do — and more. Dreams ... until Mrs Considine appears, spinning her amazing web of fantasy, creating another life for Alison out of those dreams. There is no magic in the bewitching of Alison Allbright, only the hypnotically dazzling lure of that other life. Until it's clear enough to see clearly.

STAN
Ann Pilling

Stan couldn't have been more unlucky in running away from his London foster home, for he gets unwittingly caught up in the activities of vicious criminals and is pursued by one of them who will stop at nothing to get what he wants. But throughout his terrifying journey to Warrington and Liverpool and across the Irish Sea, Stan never loses hope of the determination to find his brother and the home he dreams of.

DREAM HOUSE
Jan Mark

For Hannah, West Stenning Manor is a place of day-dreams, but for Dina its attraction lies in the celebrities who tutor the courses there. But when a well-known actor arrives, hotly pursued by his attention-seeking daughter, Julia, Dina begins to realize that famous people are no better than ordinary ones. A warm and tremendously funny story by the author of *Thunder and Lightnings*.